Al

Susie King has always loved writing stories and is highly imaginative, with a keen sense of the drama of life. Susie has been a chalet girl, daffodil picker, au pair, MP's secretary, natural health therapist and went to a convent school where she was always getting into trouble. She loves travelling, going to the movies, trees, fish & chips, snow, the sea and anything to do with space.

Dedication

To my two wonderful children, who now have children of their own.

Susie King

A Year in the Life of Rebecca Saunders

AUSTIN MACAULEY PUBLISHERS™

LONDON • CAMBRIDGE • NEW YORK • SHARJAH

Copyright © Susie King 2024

The right of Susie King to be identified as author of this work has been asserted by the author in accordance with sections 77 and 78 of the Copyright, Designs and Patents Act 1988.

All rights reserved. No part of this publication may be reproduced, stored in a retrieval system, or transmitted in any form or by any means, electronic, mechanical, photocopying, recording, or otherwise, without the prior permission of the publishers.

Any person who commits any unauthorised act in relation to this publication may be liable to criminal prosecution and civil claims for damages.

This is a work of fiction. Names, characters, businesses, places, events, locales, and incidents are either the products of the author's imagination or used in a fictitious manner. Any resemblance to actual persons, living or dead, or actual events is purely coincidental.

A CIP catalogue record for this title is available from the British Library.

ISBN 9781035838134 (Paperback)
ISBN 9781035838141 (ePub e-book)

www.austinmacauley.com

First Published 2024
Austin Macauley Publishers Ltd®
1 Canada Square
Canary Wharf
London
E14 5AA

Acknowledgements

To Clare Broadbent for all her support and encouragement and for her unwavering belief in the book.

And how shall you rise beyond your days and nights unless you break the chains which you at the dawn of your understanding have fastened around your noon hour?

In truth that which you call freedom is the strongest of these chains, though its links glitter in the sun and dazzle your eyes.

from *The Prophet* by Kahlil Gibran

Prologue

The old lady shuffled rapidly in her tattered sheepskin slippers towards the untidy pile of damp coal in the grate. She sighed deeply and hopelessly as she looked in dismay at the increasingly slender spiral of grey smoke, the colour of her hair, and swore very loudly hoping her next-door neighbour couldn't hear her forceful exclamation of failure and frustration through the thin partition wall of the little terraced house.

The dog whined pitifully from the pile of damp, smelly towels on the floor of the cold and tiny kitchen at the back of the house where she lay drying out after yet another wet walk.

And then the telephone rang stridently from its place on the old pine table next to the rusting fridge in the middle room as the old woman called it. No attempt was made to answer; she didn't feel like talking to anyone, not even to the children or to her youngest grandson who now liked to hold long, complex conversations which usually ended with her becoming gradually more and more confused about what to say and then putting down the receiver. It was the same with the children, and there seemed to her to be little point or comfort in the 'Hi! Are you OK? Yes? Oh, good! Yes, we're all fine here. The weather? Yes, it's perfect! always is Mum, you should get yourself over here one day…' calls that occurred every two weeks or so. She knew the calls were out of care and kindness but nonetheless they made her feel claustrophobic, as if trapping her inside her declining physical envelope like a helpless bird in a cage. These kind, loving calls simply made her feel old, and she resisted this feeling with all her might as if driven by some deep primeval fear of death and old age.

There were good days when she felt like her old self again—energetic, happy, possibly even optimistic—but always the dark, depressing days returned with a vengeance to merge with the night-time horrors. Last night had been a particularly bad one, and she had lain awake with her mind racing, willing a swift and painless end to her misery.

Sighing deeply again with depressed resignation, the old lady shuffled the few feet towards the storage shelves in the middle room where she reached gingerly for a wine glass sitting in isolation on the otherwise bare shelf, before bending down to retrieve from under the table a half empty bottle of cheap red wine.

She walked ponderously back towards the little low stool beside the now extinct fire, deep in thought, and sat down heavily almost toppling over backwards and nearly hitting her head on the wall behind as she clutched in desperation the glass and the bottle.

Taking a small sip of the vinegary wine and staring blankly at the grey, colourless space outside the front window, she wondered how things had got this bad, how had she sunk so low? She turned 75 this year and was desperately lonely, and had been for many years now since *… no, I won't go there, not now … I've only got myself to* *blame ... somehow I've rejected everyone and everything and ended up like this, and now there's very little left ... I will admit I do feel very lonely and afraid sometimes ... but then I've run out of everything—money, energy, even the will to survive, and I just don't think I can carry on—if only I could just slip away, in my sleep—I don't ever want the children to know this is how things are, but it's getting harder to hide it ... thank goodness they're all on the other side of the world ...*

A large tear slowly trailed a sticky path down the side of her nose, before filling the grey channel etched between her nose and the corner of her mouth, where it entered the vast pink cavern assaulting her taste-buds with the sharp tang of salt.

"Bugger everything" she sniffed forcefully, shooting a wave of salty tears into the back of her throat nearly choking in the process.

Turning her attention once more to the sooty black hole that represented her latest challenge and taking a gulp of the acidic wine, the old lady suddenly remembered a trick her father had used for resurrecting stubborn, dead fires. She carefully set down the glass and the bottle on to the grate, before reaching for last week's *Saturday Mail* lying scattered on the floor.

"Has that paper been lying there all this time?" she muttered crossly to herself as she grabbed a whole two-page sheet, ashamed at how careless and untidy she had become. Kneeling down gingerly in front of the fire, she held up the sheet of newspaper firmly over the front of the fireplace, hoping and praying that a spark remained somewhere in the solid black mess. There had been a breeze outside today which boded well for these primitive tactics. Fire lighters were too expensive and environmentally unfriendly and this simple act of defiance with the sheet of newspaper, fanned a spark of inspiration, and as the first flame flickered fragilely before exploding into life so too was her imagination and memory set alight. At last, the long dark days and nights of pain, confusion and fear, gave way to a sense of hope, determination and courage. The seed was sown.

"I will write it all down …" she vowed.

January

Becky felt the fear rising in her throat but she was powerless to do anything to prevent it as the tiny boat slithered and bucked on the crest of an enormous wave that threatened to engulf them. She sat alone in the boat on the dark, treacherous sea, except for the strange, silent man at the helm. On one side of the boat, the sea seemed to fall away into a dark, bottomless pit with jagged black rocks waiting with open jaws, but on the other side, the boiling water appeared clear and unthreatening, and in the distance Becky could make out the harbour wall, one minute seeming to be impossibly far away and the next to be within reach. On the harbour wall, stood a tall figure, silhouetted and lonely.

And then the rain came down and blotted out the tall man. Becky felt suddenly desperately alone and without hope, and instinctively knew that the little boat was set on a collision course with the cruel rocks below.

* * *

She awoke with a start and heard, as if from a long way off, the rain lashing against the old window panes. She felt terrified, still in the grips of the nightmare that had returned once again to haunt her. Becky groaned inwardly, which was worse, her recurring nightmare or the nightmare situation of her everyday world? Outside was a bleak January night with the rain tipping down and the wind howling like a banshee, no doubt ripping off the roof tiles and flinging them around like wastepaper.

Wearily Becky crawled out of the warm bed, taking care not to disturb her husband Rob who snored loudly in total oblivion. She felt a brief flash of annoyance that he could remain so blissfully unaware of the fact that she was now wide awake and that it was the middle of the night, and that she was bound to be shattered in the cold light of day.

The old house seemed to sigh and groan like a ship in a storm, and Becky had to steel herself to leave the confines of the bedroom and venture out onto the pitch-black landing.

"Damn," she swore softly as she trod on the creakiest floorboard on the entire landing that happened to be just outside Polly's bedroom. Polly slept lightly, like her mother, and would never go back to sleep if she was awakened now, in the middle of the night, by ghostly creaks and groans.

Becky held her breath for a few moments, then exhaled a sigh of relief when no answering wail came from her daughter's bedroom.

"Damn," she swore again, "where is that ruddy torch?"

William, just six, was already in the army. His whole bedroom was festooned like the inside of a soldier's tent, and of course her bedside torch always disappeared the moment William's own torch went missing.

"...story of my life," Becky grumbled as she crept across the large landing towards the head of the winding staircase. *God, what a crabby old bat I am.* she thought briefly before groping her way downstairs, tripping over her long winter nightie three steps from the bottom and slipping ungracefully onto the cold hall floor below.

"Bloody hell!" she exclaimed very loudly, still nervous after the nightmare.

No one heard or even stirred.

* * *

All the floorboards and doors creaked unbearably in the 'Old Mill House.' The sitting room door leading off the hall was the worst of all. Becky was always meaning to do something about the creaking doors, like pouring her precious, hoarded olive oil onto the ancient hinges, but of course she never got round to it.

Having successfully negotiated the obstacles in her path, Becky was now anxious to reach the confines of the warm, cosy kitchen as soon as possible; in her dream-wake state she was starting to believe that something really awful was about to happen as it frequently did in her dreams.

"Please don't wake the children," she prayed silently as she opened the kitchen door quietly. Flake and Cadbury, the family mongrels, barked in unison.

The dogs' tails thumped hard against the sides of their large, blanketed basket, but they were too snug by the Aga to venture out.

Lucky things, she thought crossly.

Then, turning on the low table lamp, Becky bent down to hug the dogs, sighing heavily, "Hello, girls, yes it is me, and it's three o'clock in the morning—would you like a biscuit?"

"Yes, please!" the tails wagged in unison.

If only my world could be contained inside this warm sanctuary, she thought as she set the heavy kettle to boil on the Aga. The wind outside was now thundering and shaking the old house, and despite its thick walls Becky wondered if, at any moment, the sea would break loose and come tearing across the marshes towards the house on the top of the hill. The children would love it. No school and playing desert islands ... rescue helicopters dropping in supplies ...

The tea made and biscuits dispensed, Becky sat curled up in her favourite chair beside the Aga. The cat, Maurice, yawned in her face from his own place of comfort beside the warm stove.

"What about the poor, wretched hens, and Polly's rabbit?" Becky panicked momentarily. But she gave in to the warmth, and sipping her tea, dismissed as impossible the thought that she might actually venture outside to check on the animals.

Outside, the hens squawked alarmingly and Paws waffled his nose rapidly, more so than usual.

The warmth of the kitchen and the even breathing of the dogs lulled Becky back into sleep. But again peace was shattered when the mug of tea slipped from her hands and crashed to the flagstone floor with a loud explosion of tinkling china. Cursing once more, Becky sat bolt upright before heaving herself out of the chair and clearing up the mess before determinedly making for the back door; here she plunged her warm bare feet into soggy, freezing cold Wellingtons and slung on her battered old Barbour, before stumbling outside via the conservatory into the wild night.

Becky made encouraging noises to the frightened rabbit in his hutch, and then groped her way towards the orchard at the back of the house and the rattling hut full of hysterical hens. She checked the doors and windows, hoping that the henhouse roof would not take off, then set off back towards the house with visions of herself clearing up the mess of uncooked scrambled eggs amongst other delights as soon as it was light.

By the time Becky returned to the kitchen, she was wide awake and her mind was buzzing. She knew it would be months, not weeks, before Rob was fit and well again. The loss of his accounts clerk job at a nearby technical college and the subsequent traumatic period of real depression, had taken its toll on them all. Even the children had become subdued, and certainly more difficult to control. Becky felt quite unashamedly desperate.

Nursing a second hot cup of tea, Becky pondered her situation and knew that she had reached a watershed and that tomorrow—no, today—she must go out and get herself a job. *It could be anything*, she thought; anything at all, from cleaning to typing, from weighing out vegetables to holding a victim's hand whilst the dentist drilled the root out of his or her inflamed jaw. As long as she was out earning during school hours, it would be something, even if it was only enough to put food on the table. Becky and Rob had just about enough funds for the moment to cope with the mortgage and other household expenses, so if she could earn something to take care of the food bills, it would make her feel she was doing something positive towards their desperate and potentially disastrous situation.

It shouldn't be difficult, she thought, but at the same time Becky knew it wasn't going to be a push-over, living as they did at the edge of the sleepy village of Little Millston, with

Crowminster 12 miles to the east and Bedhampton the same distance to the west. It just didn't seem to make sense travelling all that way just for a few hours' work—, half her pay would go on petrol for their ageing blue Renault. *It certainly won't be like falling into jobs like I did when I was in London*, Becky reflected soberly.

She stood up purposefully, made herself a cup of strong, black coffee and began scrabbling about in an old box of newspapers under the kitchen table, desperate in case she had, as usual, burnt the most up-to-date copy of the local paper instead of the most out-of-date.

"For heaven's sake, get a grip girl, get yourself organised," she muttered fiercely, scanning the 'Jobs Vacant' page of the *Western Daily Packet*. Becky had in fact browsed through the jobs section every week since Rob had lost his job, but because there was always so much else to do, it was invariably a half-hearted, 'oh well, it-can-wait-for-tomorrow,' sort of search. But now, in the depths of January and the horrendous storm, Becky knew that she must, without any further delay, take up the reins herself before they slipped into some unbearable sort of oblivion. She had very little confidence left in herself, but she would have to weather that one as she went along.

Becky glanced at the kitchen clock ticking peacefully away and saw to her surprise that it was already 6 o'clock, and although it wouldn't start to get light for a while, she managed to quietly mount the stairs and creep along to the spare bathroom at the end of the long landing to run herself a bath.

As Becky relaxed in the hot water, she felt her resolve strengthening with the promise of daylight ahead; there had been two possible job opportunities, one typing up law reports for a local solicitor and the other working for a wine importer as his secretary; there was a glimmer of hope…she would fight for her home and her family.

February

"William! please do not shout so loudly—you know daddy isn't feeling too great today."

"Charge!…" yelled William with bloodcurdling enthusiasm as he hurtled down the staircase.

"Willy, Willy," shrieked Polly, "play hostipals now, not silly soldiers!"

"No!" bellowed William from the bottom of the stairs. "Going in my jeep to see camp's OK."

"No! no! no!" screamed Polly.

"ENOUGH! BOTH OF YOU!" yelled Becky at the top of her voice, "Come into the kitchen *immediately*."

William sheepishly, but with a touch of rebellion, said quietly, "Snot fair, Mum, I've been stuck in all day 'n I want to go out—Polly's *boring*, she won't be killed…"

"Want to be alive nurse not dead one," sniffed Polly loudly, dragging her stuffed chicken behind her as she shuffled slowly into the kitchen.

"Children," said Becky kindly but firmly, "now I know things aren't easy at the moment with poor Daddy unwell and Mummy working all the time and getting cross all the time, but we need to *help* each other right now. So, what you are both going to do is to play *quietly* until suppertime! OK?"

Both children stood staring at her, as if transfixed by a ghost.

"On the other hand," continued Becky, pretending not to notice, "we could always ask Miss Clasby to give you both some work to do at home after school, couldn't we?"

Her last comment hung in the air for no more than a second, both children stared at Becky as if she really was an alien before rapidly disappearing in different directions, Polly to take Paws for a walk on a lead around the conservatory, and William to pelt down the drive on his bike to his camp hidden amongst the soggy undergrowth beneath damp, dripping trees.

"God I need a drink," muttered Becky as she returned to the kitchen having 'tucked up' the hens for the night. The dregs of last night's bottle of red plonk stood uncorked by the sink. She poured the wine into one of the last remaining crystal wine glasses and took a desperate gulp.

"Now, food…that'll make us all feel better," she said to herself and the resident audience of Maurice, Flake and Cadbury, who miaowed and wagged their tails respectively. Becky opened wide the large store cupboard which revealed not a lot. A few tins of baked beans, some dried macaroni, masses of brown rice (which she was always buying because she felt it was good for them but which Rob and the children turned their noses up at), a tin of coconut milk, tinned frankfurters, tinned pineapple, and cake-making ingredients in abundance although Becky rarely made cakes as everyone preferred hot buttered toast and marmite for tea.

With a sigh, Becky took the macaroni and a tin of baked beans from the cupboard, before wandering over to inspect the contents of the fridge.

"Lucky this time," she said wryly as she spied some cheese, a couple of pieces of pale-looking streaky bacon, and a distinctly limp lettuce.

"Macaroni cheese with a difference or lump it," she said to her blinking audience, and proceeded to chop one of the last remaining home-grown onions with her sharp kitchen knife as if cutting up a mortal enemy.

Into the bottom oven of the Aga went the macaroni, followed by an earthenware dish bulging with green Brambly apples covered with the last of the brown sugar. She would worry about what they were going to eat tomorrow, tomorrow.

It was getting dark outside as the music for the Flintstones, current favourite DVD, blasted through the kitchen wall from the sitting room next door. Polly must have bored with the rabbit circus game she had been playing with Paws in the conservatory.

"Hi, anything I can do?"

Startled and guilty, Becky spun round from her reverie at the sink as glass in hand she found Rob standing and staring at her from the kitchen door. It was, as ever, a statement rather than a question of intent to help. She sighed and answered Rob's half-hearted gesture, muttering, "No, it's OK, thanks," knowing that he was far more interested in Fred and Thelma's domestic crises than their own.

Walking swiftly across the kitchen to the back door, Becky plunged her feet into her Wellington boots, the dogs nearly knocking her to the ground in their excitement and anticipation of a twilight walk, before shouting over her shoulder,

"Supper's nearly ready, I'm just off to find Wills…back in a minute…"

But her words were addressed to empty space as Rob had already wandered back into the sitting room to the comfort of the fire, the sofa and the television.

"Why the hell didn't I get him to go searching for William? And why didn't I ask him to check the fire…?" She muttered to herself, knowing full well that only she fed the open log fire that crackled warmly in the grate; and with these thoughts, Becky banged grumpily out of the house.

"William," she said firmly and marched off in search of her errant son, Flake and Cadbury bounding ahead into the dusk.

Meanwhile, Polly was playing a circus game with her rabbit, oblivious of the fact that Maurice was watching discreetly as he cleaned his face with his paws in the doorway leading into the conservatory, his half-closed eyes from time to time focussing intently on the innocent bundle of soft fur.

* * *

Supper, as usual, was a strained affair, with them all seated around the scrubbed oak kitchen table. Polly sat on her chair humming, in her own dream world, not concentrating one bit on the job in hand, much to her mother's annoyance and frustration. William on the other hand had wolfed down his macaroni *alla beans* and now sat looking bored, his mouth ringed with tomato ketchup. Rob sat quietly, eating slowly, and saying nothing. Becky also was silent.

This is getting beyond a joke, she thought, *something will have to change around here or I will literally go up in smoke.*

The ordeal of the mealtime over, the rest of the family somehow spirited themselves away with amazing speed and stealth from the debris in the kitchen, and were ensconced once more in front of the flickering box, this time watching what sounded like a programme about a family of ghouls. Feeling as if she could very easily curl up and either sleep for a year or die, Becky wearily plunged her arms into the suds of the washing up bowl, and slowly but surely until they formed a torrent down both sides of her nose, her tears fell.

"It's no good, I can't stand it anymore," she inwardly screamed, sobbing quietly. And then the thought hit her like a bolt, disappearing as fast as it had appeared...*perhaps he'd sit up and take notice if I jumped off the roof or swallowed a bottle of aspirin or something...*

Collapsing in a heap in her chair beside the Aga, Becky was genuinely frightened at her own state of mind. *How in God's name did I ever get to thinking like that? Self-pity, that's what it is, and there is absolutely no one I can talk to ...*' her thoughts rambled on desperately, *...and I can't ring Mum, I'd just start blabbing down the phone and that would mean two of us hysterical...*'

Liza and Bill Copeland, Becky's mother and father, lived about ten miles away in Claymoor St John, but Becky knew that however desperate she was, she could not at the moment ring her parents and unload; her father was just getting going again after a hip replacement last year and all her mother's energies were centred on him '...*no, it just wouldn't be fair, or right*,' she concluded firmly.

"What about Vicky, Caroline and Ginny?" Becky brightened momentarily as she recalled her ex-London flatmates, and then her mood plummeted again as she recalled that her so-called closest friends were all still zooming around London leading their hectic lives, and that in reality, they were now too far removed from her seemingly cosy, country existence and did not merit a hysterical, soul-searching phone call from her concerning a husband they hardly knew.

March

"Wake up, you dozey woman!" bellowed Leo from his end of the tiny attic office.

"What the hell's got into you? This is the *third* time this week you've crashed out on me, and it's only Tuesday for Chrissake!"

"…just another night without a decent sleep…" yawned Becky.

"Not my problem, girl, you're here to do a job of work not catch up on your beauty sleep. And by the way, when Pierre gets here for the tasting, I want you in tip-top form—and you'd better not even think of sticking your nose in a glass—can't risk you becoming intoxicated even with alcohol fumes in your present state—someone's got to stay intact and sober. Email him that list of samples to bring with him will you? And while you're at it, get us both a strong black coffee—makes me want to pass out just looking at you."

"By the way," Leo shouted at Becky, exiting the office at speed, "get yourself a bit spruced up for when he's here—turn on the sex appeal a bit…you may want to put in some practice…"

Becky blinked mutely after Leo as Flake and Cadbury banged their tails on the floor from their place under her desk, in innocent praise of the obviously well-deserved congratulations which had just been heaped upon their mistress by the retreating Leo.

* * *

The contrast of Leo to Rob ensured that, for the most part, Becky enjoyed her work. Leo was never quiet, never still and always bursting with enthusiasm over some unpronounceable wine or other. Leo was renowned and respected for his excellent albeit red-tipped 'nose'. His large, aquiline beak brought people flocking from miles around to sample and purchase cases of his imported nectar. A rambling old house was where he lived and ran his wine business from. The Old Manor was situated in the centre of the picturesque, timeless village of Little Beresford, next to the tiny eleventh century grey stone church. Leo's wife Fizz was notorious as the best fund-raiser in the county. Fizz had two pet charities, one aiding starving children in Africa where she was born, and the other a charity providing support for the terminally ill. She was totally ruthless when it came to donations and supplies for raffles from her husband's wine cellars. Tea parties and garden fetes were held in the beautiful manor grounds, and on occasions there were known to be queues of impatient cars outside the garden walls, waiting to gain entry for cream teas and cases of Chateauneuf-du-Pape and Oppenheimer Krotenbrunnen!

The work for Becky was not onerous and she just soaked up the energy and enthusiasm that charged Leo and Fizz as if drinking from a cool fountain in a desert oasis. Becky felt guilty about her exhausted state, and made a mental note to maybe enlist Fizz's sympathetic ear when their paths next crossed and perhaps explain tactfully that she did have a few minor problems to cope with at home which would, of course, blow over shortly. It would be worse than useless to say anything to Leo about her difficulties in explanation for her current 'dozey' state of mind!

The exotic smell of coffee from the filter machine brought Becky out of her reverie—that and the energetic thud of Leo's returning footsteps.

"Right, noses to the grindstone! And that excludes you two mutts under the table!"

* * *

Since coming to work for Leo a few weeks ago, Becky's confidence had risen a few degrees as she gradually recognised that she was not quite as hopeless and scatterbrained as she had come to believe. She could still type very fast, take down shorthand when needed, send emails, and also talked with confidence now on the office telephone. She was no longer nervous that whatever she said would sound foolish and unsophisticated. Becky knew she was picking up the threads of her life again, and as her confidence and self-esteem seeped back, she became a more patient and understanding person.

Rob however had seemingly drifted without struggle into the role of house-husband. The only difference, however, was that unlike most house-husbands, Rob lifted not a single finger to help in the running of the household or in the care of the children—except for one concession; precisely on the dot of 3.15 every afternoon, he set off from home to walk to the village school ten minutes away in time to collect Polly and William, walk them home again arriving in time for the three of them to plonk down in front of children's television, munching crisps and sweets until Becky came home at 5.

Becky regularly returned home with a bottle of wine from work, usually plonked on her desk by Leo with a demand that she give it her verdict.

Tonight though Becky tried to let this all go over the top of her head as wine glass in hand, wooden spoon in the other stirring the pot, she fought to retain her newly acquired confidence and sense of self-esteem.

"What's for nosh Mum? I'm *starving*!" announced William, sloping into the kitchen, his school uniform awry and mud caked on his grey trousers.

"Spag bog, French bread, salad, and fruit!" replied Becky brightly from her station at the Aga.

"But Muuum, we had that yesterday," moaned William.

"Never mind, darling, it's good for you and it's different today because it's a vege spag bog!"

"Yuck," was the retreating reply, "I hate it without meat!"

"No you don't poppet!" Becky called after him, pausing in her vigorous stirrings to take a large gulp of Cotes du Rhone Villages. "Off you go now and wash your hands, supper's ready, and tell Polly and Daddy to do the same."

It was Wednesday, and about four weeks to go before the children broke up; Easter was quite early this year. Becky took each day as it came, blandly ignoring the fact that the holidays were actually approaching and that problems would be sure to arise. Weekends certainly gave her insight as to what joys lay ahead and as a result, each

Monday morning as she wearily dragged herself into work, feeling like a soldier who had just waded through the mud of the Somme, she mentally switched off the advancing horrors.

April

Large, round, wet tears poured down Jemma Watkins' red cheeks. She blinked rapidly and with increasing panic as her tears mingled on her once neat English composition book with the drops of ink that had suddenly and inexplicably appeared from nowhere on the page. Jemma sobbed very loudly as she realised she had completely lost the thread of the story she had been so engrossed in writing, all about the woodland adventures of her cat Thomasina.

"Jemma dear, what on earth is the matter?" Miss Clasby said from the front of the classroom. The whole class stopped writing and turned around to stare at Jemma, which only served to increase her noisy distress. Quickly, Miss Clasby walked between the rows of desks to where the sobbing little girl sat one row from the back.

"What on earth is going on?" she demanded, sternly surveying the children who sat nearest to Jemma. All the children thus interrogated dumbly shook their heads, with the exception of the little boy who sat directly behind Jemma and who now had his head not six inches from his work book, pen in hand, tongue stuck resolutely out of one corner of his mouth in a show of extreme concentration, his cheeks apparently red with effort!

"William Saunders, what is the meaning of all this?" Miss Clasby said, now quite angry and clearly flustered. "Stand up immediately, put down your pen, look at me, and explain to me please," continued the elderly form teacher.

After a slight pause, William slowly stood up and clearing his throat said in a voice totally devoid of any form of regret and not without a touch of indignation,

"Well, Miss, she's been shot you see! Look, she's been shot in the back and now she's bleeding all over the place!"

With a feeling approaching total horror and amidst stifled sniggers from the rest of the class, Miss Clasby leaned forwards to peer at Jemma's back. The little girl's blouse was splattered with royal blue ink, washable she hoped, and some of this visual-effect material had obviously overshot the mark and landed upon Jemma's neatly written composition.

Oh Lord, groaned Miss Clasby inwardly. *This is the third time in a fortnight that William has disgraced himself. He's always been such a good little boy, until now that is… I must, without fail, catch his parents today and have a word with them.*

"William and Jemma, come with me a moment," said Miss Clasby briskly as she made her way back to her desk at the front of the classroom. "And Jemma, put on your pullover. Now, the rest of you, back to your work and not a squeak out of *anyone*."

Sitting down at her desk rather heavily, Miss Clasby looked at the two children over the top of her glasses.

"William, I need hardly tell you this is extremely serious. Now, please make a nice apology to poor Jemma. And you will immediately write a letter saying how sorry you are to Jemma's mother which you will hand to her at the end of the day—I shall be there to make sure that you do!" said Miss Clasby very firmly.

She then looked hard at William, who in turn spoke, none too apologetically, to Jemma, "Sorrreee Jemma for all the mess and stuff, twon't happen again…but I really, really was crawling along and then…" William's face lit up as he turned to his form teacher excitedly.

"That's enough William!" Miss Clasby almost shouted. She had never shouted at anyone or anything in her whole life; this whole scenario was shocking indeed. " Now, back to your places both of you," she continued more calmly, "and Jemma dear, do try to cheer up, and don't worry I shall talk to your mother later."

Poor Jemma was still upset, if not a little confused, and kept sniffing and wiping her nose on the back of her sleeve.

When all was quiet once more, Miss Clasby admitted to herself with a deep sigh that this time Headmaster would have to be informed. She would like to have dealt with this in her own way but school rules were made not to be broken, and the current situation required reporting the matter to the Headmaster. Mr Faulkner was a force to be reckoned with at the best of times, and unfortunately was not blessed with a compassionate nature. He was a hard man with a total sense of humour failure.

The dinner bell sounded as William and Miss Clasby waited outside Headmaster's study. Miss Clasby knocked firmly on the door with a look of resolve lending strength to her tired features.

"Come!" was the instant response.

"Ah, Miss Clasby, and William Saunders I see," intoned Headmaster, fixing the pair with a glassy, dark glare.

"Miss Clasby informs me that you behaved in an extremely unruly manner in class this morning, William. Explain pleash," continued Headmaster, showering his blotting pad with spittle.

"Well, sir, it was like this you see," William began bravely and earnestly, "...I was craw..."

"What William means, sir", interrupted Miss Clasby loudly and swiftly before William could say another word, "is that he was attempting to get his pen to write, after refilling it, by giving it a little shake, when most unfortunately the ink shot out all over the place and in particular all over Jemma Thomas's back!"

William gawped open-mouthed up at Miss Clasby as she continued rapidly, again leaving no room for any interruptions.

"William is extremely sorry for all the trouble he has caused and has written a very nice letter to Jemma's mother which he has here to show to you Headmaster!" she finished with a flourish.

"William?" Miss Clasby sharply urged.

"Oh...yes...smy letter, Sir..." William said very slowly and quietly. "Sorry...I didn't *mean* to make Jemma's back all messy...it just sort of slipped...like stuff *does* specially when..."

William's voice began to get louder as he once again warmed to his subject. The captive audience *must* hear all about his exciting, bloodcurdling adventure! The underworld took over again!

"William Shaunders!" showered Mr Faulkner through gritted, yellow teeth, his smooth, sleeked-back shock of grey hair instantly becoming dishevelled as his head shot forwards towards William's now astonished face. Headmaster wore a somewhat wild look in his eye—William stood transfixed as Mr Faulkner's left eyeball swivelled angrily on a totally different elliptical path to his right eyeball!

Miss Clasby, paralysed like a rabbit caught in the glare of car headlights by this unfortunate turn of events, was shocked back into action at the sight of William's awestruck expression which was totally devoid of fear or remorse.

William opened his mouth. He wanted very badly to comment on the extraordinary sight of Headmaster frothing at the mouth with his eyeballs awry!

"William, I think it would be best if you waited for me outside the door a moment please!" Miss Clasby very rapidly and very loudly intoned.

William's eyebrows shot up as if in surprise, then slowly, as he backed out of the room, he lowered his left eyebrow raising the right one simultaneously, giving the distinct impression that he was observing the actions of a mad man.

"Phew!" he said to himself as he slumped down on the wooden bench outside Mr Faulkner's study door. An alien life-form had obligingly introduced itself into William's world. The possibilities were endless! William felt hugely pleased with himself and the way things were progressing, as far as his private army was concerned that is.

Five minutes later, Miss Clasby emerged from Headmaster's study, two bright red spots glowed starkly on her plump, hairy cheeks.

"You will sit next to me at dinner, William," she said abruptly as if from a long way off.

"Smells like fish fingers n' chips!" chirped William cheerfully as they set off down the corridor towards the dining room. Miss Clasby did not respond.

Back in the classroom after dinner break, William was to be found tongue lolling out of the side of his mouth, drawing pictures of imaginary soldiers on a large piece of snowy white paper. He was seated at the left-hand side of Miss Clasby's desk away from the rest of the class, and Jemma.

End of school bell rang at last, and scraping his chair loudly on the floor, causing his teacher to wince, William immediately stood to attention, his classmates giggling nervously. William was a hero by now, although he was entirely unaware of this fact!

After the usual end of school hymn and prayer—"Now the day is over…" hummed William not remembering the words—"Our Father who art in heaven…" he remembered that first line especially because it seemed to him a very odd thing to say when his father was waiting at the school gates to take him and Polly home. Miss Clasby dismissed her class, firmly holding William's hand to make sure he didn't escape.

"Can I go now, please?" William asked earnestly, looking up at his form mistress.

"Yes, but I am coming with you," said Miss Clasby quite kindly. "I would just like to have a word with your parents, and I hope you haven't forgotten that you need to see Jemma's mother and give her your letter."

"We must be quick though," said William breathlessly, "or Polly and Dad won't wait and I'll miss out on sweets 'n' things!"

By now they were standing by the cloakroom door. William grabbed his dark blue duffle coat and rushed out into the playground like a launched torpedo before Miss Clasby could stop him.

"Dad! Dad!" yelled William rushing up to where Rob and Polly stood waiting for him.

"Wow, I've seen an alien today!" His face glowing with excitement, William screeched to a halt.

"Don't be tho thilly Wills," said Polly briefly, immediately returning her thumb to her mouth and looking up at Rob with eyebrows raised.

Rob stood silently, first gazing blankly at his wayward son, before equally blankly staring at the sight of Miss Clasby sailing across the playground towards them like a fully rigged galleon.

"Ahh…Mr Saunders…and Polly!" gasped Miss Clasby breathlessly, feeling quite definitely that in all her 45 years of primary school life, today had to be the very worst day of all. Her natural composure and sense of decorum had totally vanished out of the window. It was obvious that Headmaster had also suffered the same fate. She was dreading the meeting that would inevitably ensue after the culprit's departure through the school gates.

"Mr Saunders, may I have a brief word with you please? …but first of all, William come with me just a moment, there is Jemma's mother and you must give her your letter."

Taking William firmly by the hand, Miss Clasby sailed rapidly towards Mrs Thomas. Turning his face up to Jemma's mother, William smiled broadly before handing her his letter. Miss Clasby gave Mrs Thomas a brief rundown of events, whilst William stood imprisoned in his form teacher's grip, staring non-committally at a silent and slightly sulky-looking Jemma. *What's up with her?* William wondered.

"Now!" said Miss Clasby in as positive a tone as she could muster as she and William rejoined Rob and Polly. "William! Polly! Would you just both please stand together here a few moments whilst your father and I have a little chat? And please do not move!" she added for good measure, in as firm a tone as possible.

William and Polly nodded slowly and in unison as if weighing up someone who had definitely 'lost the plot!'

Placing her right hand gently but firmly under Rob's right elbow, Miss Clasby attempted to swivel Rob's vision away from the children towards a different angle, before guiding him three steps away from the waiting pair.

"Mr Saunders," Miss Clasby said breathlessly, her tone hissing slightly, just above a whisper.

"What?" Rob said quite loudly, and quite rudely thought Miss Clasby.

"I'm very concerned about William…" she ventured, hoping desperately to illicit a parental response from William and Polly's silent father, concern, some kind of rapport, even anxiety maybe, if nothing else that she herself was so obviously in a high state of stress due to as yet unrevealed events of the day.

But no, nothing. No response. With a mounting sense of panic, Miss Clasby realised she was communicating with someone bordering on a zombie. Drawing on all her considerable inner reserves of strength and resolve, William's form teacher heard herself saying in a loud voice so that William could also hear,

"…as we're so near the end of term, I feel William would benefit from a few extra days' holiday! He is obviously over-tired. So, I won't expect him back until the beginning of the summer term! Mr Saunders?"

"Yup," was the only response Miss Clasby elicited from the father, as he continued looking at her with his blank expression.

I really think he believes I've gone mad, thought the form teacher desperately, but then as if a light had suddenly been switched on in a very dark room, through the layers of trauma and stress of the day, Miss Clasby was hit as if by a blinding light. The problem lay not with William but with the father.

Is he on drugs? she pondered suspiciously.

Miss Clasby knew that the mother, Mrs Saunders, had recently stopped bringing the children to school and collecting them at the end of the day.

Ah! This must be it! she thought, *the husband is out of work and is acting as house-husband whilst the mother goes out to work … of course, why didn't I think of it before … a little family having a few problems … but made all the worse because the father is behaving so strangely …*

Miss Clasby made a mental note to keep a very close eye on these two young children next term, and she would of course inform Polly's form mistress, Mrs Hitchens.

Her swift reverie was loudly interrupted by a wail of distress from Polly who was clearly very upset that her brother was to have more holiday than her.

"Snot fair," blubbed Polly, Wills gaping at her in surprise. This was his treat, his reward for going into battle—what'd it got to do with his sister he wondered. Then Wills' mouth sagged at the edges as he too began to howl!

Desperately looking around to see who was watching, Miss Clasby quickly surrounded the two children with her arms and ample bosom.

"There, there, my dears, I think it's time to go home now don't you? I'll have a word with Mrs Hitchens, Polly, so don't worry, just have a lovely Easter holiday both of you and come back next term all bright-eyed and bushy-tailed!" she clucked kindly. "You can all go home now."

Both children looked red-eyed at the kind old lady with her white bun all askew and little wispy, twiggy bits sticking out all over the place, and began to giggle nervously.

Pinkly, Miss Clasby stood up and facing Rob said quite loudly, "You can go home now Mr Saunders. Why don't you take William and Polly into the corner shop and let them choose some sweeties?"

It flitted through Miss Clasby's mind that she was now talking to three children instead of two. Rob merely nodded, and with a bouncing, leaping child in either hand, turned and crossed the road without a backward look or word of thanks. All three vanished into the sweet shop as if by magic!

Exhausted, Miss Clasby turned back to face the school building and with heavy steps plodded in that direction, uncertain of what awaited her and if anything remained of headmaster. But she would talk to Mrs Hitchens first, and give herself a little time to gather up her waning senses, over a hot, sweet cup of tea she hoped.

May

Becky happened to be glancing out of the attic office window when she spied a sleek, silver grey Mercedes Convertible sliding through the entrance gates to the Old Manor. Her pulse momentarily quickened, she had not expected Pierre to arrive in such style; she mentally scanned herself in her small handbag mirror—no lipstick on front teeth, no biscuit crumbs lurking at corners of mouth, and yes, another squirt of Airwaves breath freshener. Becky smoothed the imaginary creases in her tight red skirt, checked under the arms of the red silk blouse for any damp patches, and put her hands nervously up to her glossy black hair.

Becky could hear Leo's booming voice welcoming the Frenchman through his portals, followed by Fizz's piercing trill.

"Becky! Come down here at once. Pierre 'est arrive'!" Leo shouted pompously up the two flights of stairs.

'Right, this is where the real work begins', mused Becky, stepping nervously on to the small landing outside the office at the top of the winding staircase. A sudden thought brought about a flash of panic that nearly threw her off balance as she teetered on the edge of the stairs as a vision of Flash and Cadbury gasping for air in the car

flooded her mind … '*No, I left the front windows open a couple of inches I'm sure I did … didn't I? yes I definitely must have done*'. But the thought had unnerved Becky, robbing her of the minute ray of self-esteem and self-confidence that had taken hours, in fact days, to generate.

Halfway downstairs, pausing on the bedroom floor landing, Becky once again checked her appearance, at the same time mentally banishing thoughts of the dogs, before proceeding to step as confidently as possible on to the flight of stairs winding down to the little group waiting below in the large, open hallway.

Leo, Fizz and Pierre stopped talking and looked up as Becky began her descent; she imagined this must be how those skinny supermodels felt as they stepped out onto the catwalk, preparing to sashay and strut. Three steps from ground floor level however, Becky faltered and lost her composure as she felt her left ankle give way under the strain of remaining cool whilst balancing atop six-inch heels. She landed with a thud on the stairs, and with legs askew sat staring at the three aghast faces gaping at her sudden demise.

Leo, quick as ever on the uptake, moved rapidly towards Becky before yanking her onto her feet again, making 'there, there' noises and whisking her down the remaining three stairs rapidly and firmly.

"Pierre, mon ami, this is Becky the secretary!" Leo said loudly, adding in a broadside to Becky with a glint in his eye of what she was not quite sure, "arriving in style as usual!"

Fizz took over from Leo, steering a puzzled looking Pierre away from the embarrassing scene of disaster towards the large drawing room where awaited them polished and sparkling crystal flutes and a jeroboam of Leo's finest champagne from the cellars below, chilling in a large silver ice bucket.

"Darling, you do the honours," drawled Fizz, "and Pierre, come and sit down, here next to me" she ordered, patting the luxurious cushions scattered about the large cream sofa.

Leo, puffing and panting slightly, turned to Becky and intoning in his most polite, silky voice, exhaled, "Becky, be so good as to hand the glasses around. *And for Chrissake don't drop anything or do anything stupid"* he hissed out of the side of his bewhiskered mouth.

Becky's dark eyes momentarily blinked wide-open in surprise as she was struck with a sense of being a rabbit caught in the headlights of a ten-ton truck on a dark night, before a feeling of detachment and haughty indifference took over. Her confidence flooded back, and she was fired up with anger and a sense of injustice at Leo's unruly behaviour. Becky omitted to acknowledge, in her relief at feeling her confidence return, that in fact Leo had saved the day by covering up for her clumsy entrance.

"Pierre" Becky silked, bending over and revealing her cleavage, "a glass of 1983 Dom Perignon? You've had a long journey; you can relax now!" she continued, smiling at the very handsome, dark-haired Frenchman whilst struggling to maintain her composure. There was no hiding the fact that there was an instant flash of magnetic attraction as their eyes locked, momentarily threatening to turn Becky's knees to jelly. Regaining her cool however, Becky smiled again at Pierre as sexily as she could before easing her way back to the champagne bottles being held by an open-mouthed Leo.

"Er, yes, of course, Pierre, mais oui, relax, enjoy, salut and all that" he muttered, glowering at Becky as he handed her a glass of the honey-coloured gently fizzing nectar for his wife.

"Darling Becky, thank you sooo much! Now, Pierre ..." Fizz continued, turning swiftly and elegantly towards him, "tell me all about your journey, was it beastly? And how are the children ..." she prattled on.

"Feeling alright now are we?" Leo hissed in an aside to Becky as she returned to the champagne bottle and the two remaining flutes, as if he wasn't yet quite sure whether he could trust her or not to make another blunder.

"Absolutely fine thank you Leo, never better!" Becky replied loudly, already tipsy from the smell of the champagne and the memory of Pierre's dark eyes searching her own.

Leo glowered, and then finally relaxed, throwing himself into a deeply cushioned soft leather armchair next to Fizz and opposite to Pierre.

"Becky, sit." he said motioning to a multi-coloured pouffe next to him. Becky sat obediently feeling more dog-like than she cared to admit. But as she sipped the exquisite nectar, she closed her eyes and prepared to transport herself to champagne heaven, only to open them again briefly and find Pierre's piercing gaze fixated on the area just above her left breast.

Slowly Becky came out of her reverie whilst cautiously moving her eyes away from Pierre's face and looking as surreptitiously as possible in the direction of his fixed gaze.

She gasped very loudly on a sharp intake of breath, for there pinioned in full glory on her blouse for all the world to see, unnoticed until now by Leo or Fizz who had been too distracted by her unfortunate entrance and the entertainment of Pierre, was a badge, a remnant of a girls' night out a few weeks back with a group of school mums, with the upside down words 'I'm Horny And Wanna Get Laid' staring her in the face.

Slowly, a dark red blush spread upwards from Becky's exposed chest to her neck, until her entire face was on fire. She stood up suddenly and, summoning every ounce of her composure, announced that she must fly away immediately to attend to the dogs, the chickens, the children, the rabbit. Becky's exit route beckoned more clearly with each passing second and her flimsy composure gained full strength as she took charge of the situation. Standing resolutely, Becky held out a steady hand to Pierre in a gesture of farewell, before swiftly bidding goodnight and thank you to a speechless Leo and Fizz, and then vanishing as if into thin air, banging the front door loudly on the way out.

"Well!" said Fizz exhaling vehemently. "Now, where were we Pierre?" she continued tight-lipped turning her full attention back to the astonished Frenchman, temporarily excluding Leo from the picture, whom she briefly noticed was for once struck dumb!

* * *

"Well, that's completely and utterly blown it," muttered Becky as she made her way quickly to the car. "Messed up my job, which may be just as well, Pierre was so good looking in a dark, Mediterranean, Corsican-bandit sort of way…"

Becky vividly remembered that those eyes of his on her face had been like a caress.

"No wonder I fell down the stairs!" she said crossly, recalling the excruciating scene earlier.

"Must think I'm a complete idiot, and what about the bloody badge!" she groaned. "Oh damn it, I didn't even notice it was there, he must think I'm a tart or a trollop or whatever it is they call them in France."

By the time she reached the car, Becky had composed herself sufficiently to be able to begin the half hour's drive home safely, having thrown open the side windows in the back of the car for the dogs to drool out of. She had been relieved to know she hadn't gone completely potty when she found a well-aired car and two patiently-waiting dogs. But nonetheless, she was very steamed up.

Speeding down the drive and scattering gravel onto the immaculate lawns, from her position in the driver's seat, Becky yelled, "Shit!" very loudly at the top of her voice, whilst clutching the steering wheel with both hands simultaneously until her knuckles went white. Flake and Cadbury jumped visibly, before flattening themselves on the backseat as the car shot onto the main road.

"Why do I always make a complete mess of everything!" she shouted out of the open car window to the dusk outside and a field of cows surprised out of their regurgitating reveries.

Luckily for Becky, she was not 'over the limit,' either in speed or alcohol as the police car with flashing lights slid alongside the little red car at Postgate Roundabout. The window on the driver's side was open anyway as the nearside officer mouthed to her through his own opening window 'to open hers.' Becky inwardly groaned as she viewed the scene unfolding as if from a great distance, rather like one of those out-of-body experiences she was always reading about – people on the operating table hovering at ceiling height, observing the gory carnage below. From her distant viewpoint, she heard the vibes of Dark Side of the Moon wailing at high volume, together with Flake and Cadbury's rejoining howls from the back seat.

The police officer handed Becky a note that read 'pull over next pull in,' and with that, the flashing white car sped sleekly away westwards as the roundabout traffic cleared. Becky was left open-mouthed and flustered as a line of honking cars queued up behind her.

"Shit!" she said, again, more quietly this time, as she too moved onto the roundabout and towards her assignation.

* * *

Half a mile further down the dual-carriageway, Becky began to indicate left; flashing police car lights lit up the sky.

"Shit again," she murmured as she came to a standstill behind WY339POL. Flake and Cadbury's vocal chords gained strength once more as PC1096 approached the car.

"Everything alright miss?" he shouted, standing well clear but within earshot of the vibrating car.

"Yes. Fine. Thank you!" Becky shouted over the din of howling dogs and music, groping to turn off the CD.

With noise levels slightly reduced, the policeman ventured a step towards the car, holding out the dreaded breathalyser.

"Care to blow into this for me miss?" he shouted.

"Of course!" Becky shouted back, all at once annoyed, the events of the entire day exploding in her head. "And there's no need to shout, I'm not deaf," she yelled furiously.

'I'll show these smart-arses where to get off, they think I'm a drunk driver,' Becky thought angrily as she blew vigorously into the breathalyser.

"That's fine thank you miss. Got far to go have you? No? Well off you go then, dogs need feeding by the looks of 'em. Goodnight miss." And quick as a flash, before Becky could say a word, the police car swooshed off at speed into the gathering dusk.

A shocked Becky holding phone away from her ear, hair standing on end.

* * *

Supper that night was a disastrous affair. The cupboards were bare, yet again, as Becky slipped on her apron remembering with a sinking heart that in the aftermath of her journey home and her brief encounter with the dark-eyed Pierre, she had totally forgotten to stop by at the Co-Op for food. Pressing her knuckles hard into her temples, she fought back tears of frustration as she struggled to regain her composure.

Soon her indomitable resources came to the rescue as she slipped out of the house, and headed for the chicken shed. Collecting six eggs from beneath the indignant hens who had already settled their feathers for the night, she placed them carefully into her apron pockets before heading to the greenhouse. Here, she rummaged around until she had gleaned a few old potatoes stored in a damp sack together with some mouldy looking carrots and one withered onion.

Returning to the house, Becky found half a packet of peas and some sliced mushrooms buried beneath snow ice at the bottom of the empty freezer. Breathing a sigh of relief that sustenance, albeit of a dubious sort, was in the offing, Becky turned her attention to the bottle of 1993 Beaujolais Villages sitting on the kitchen table.

The wine open, cork dispensed, Becky settled herself for a moment's respite in her chair by the Aga, full glass in hand. All was quiet, except for the occasional bloodcurdling yell from the sitting room where Rob and the children were sitting as if hypnotised in front of the television. The glare from the screen flickered like lightning.

"Bloody hell," exhaled Becky to the ménage-a-trois watching her patiently with adoring, if sceptical, expressions.

Half an hour later, as Flake and Cadbury harmoniously clattered their metal feeding bowls, now empty, around the kitchen floor, and Maurice sat neatly cleaning his whiskers by the back door, Becky set about creating a meal out of her obscure ingredients, feeling quite drunk after two glasses of the red wine. Hiccoughing loudly, she stood at the old sink preparing the vegetables. These she then proceeded to parboil before flinging them into the large heavy pan on the Aga with the last of the olive oil and the frozen vegetables, until a distinctly dubious mush appeared. Cracking the eggs into a basin, Becky beat them hard with a fork taking out the day's frustrations with a vengeance on the unsuspecting ingredients. Adding salt and pepper, she poured the eggs with flourish onto the sizzling vegetables.

Three minutes later, Becky yelled into thin air, "Supper!"

Five minutes later, as Becky sat fork in hand ready to attack her food, her family trouped in, Rob last of all.

Wills exclaimed excitedly as he sat down "Mum, I'm on holidays!"

"Me too!" shouted Polly dancing around the kitchen.

"Yuk. Where's the ketchup?" Wills said rudely, peering closely at his plate.

"There isn't any," said Becky coldly. "And what do you mean you're on holiday? School doesn't finish until Thursday and it's only Monday today."

In unison, William and Polly shouted, "We've been given extra holidays!"

"For being very good!" added Wills smugly.

Becky looked in astonishment at Rob, waiting for some kind of response, but his head was bent over his plate as he rapidly shovelled food into his mouth.

"Rob!" said Becky loudly. "What is the meaning of this?"

Rob merely shrugged and picking up his empty plate, shuffled over to the sink, chucking it into the soapy water before moving quickly across the kitchen floor towards the comforts of the sitting room, leaving an open-mouthed Becky with her fork poised in the air. Her food dropped onto the table as she struggled to maintain her tattered composure.

"Blast," she said vehemently. Then gathering up her waning senses, Becky held out both arms to her children.

"Darlings, what is going on?…" But before she could continue, Wills butted in, "Mummy, it's been a reelly, reelly good day 'n I'm so happy!" and sighing contentedly, he proceeded to sit down and eat everything on his plate for once not complaining.

"Polly?" Becky said weakly, "What's happened?"

"Well Mummy," said Polly comfortingly, "Wills was very good at school today. He saw Mr Frog, and Miss Clasby told us we could have extra holidays. Isn't that lovely?" she added dreamily.

Becky said nothing, and the three of them sat calmly together until all plates were empty.

"Now off you go my loves, I need to talk to Daddy" said Becky lightly.

Jumping up and down, Polly and Wills hugged Becky excitedly before becoming aeroplanes and swooping gleefully in the direction of the television, where a few moments later Becky found a sultry, distant Rob sitting as in a trance.

"Robert!" Becky said loudly. Rob's head jerked up momentarily before returning his gaze to the screen, muttering, "What?"

At that moment, the telephone shrilled in Becky's left ear, rendering her temporarily stunned.

"Becky! Becky!" shrieked a female voice. "Is that you?" The shriek transformed into an exquisitely painful high-pitched wail. Instantly, Becky recognised Rob's sister Chloe.

"Becky, Becky, I need to speak to Rob, NOW!" Chloe's voice quivered.

Stunned momentarily, Becky gaped for a few seconds at the receiver, before shaking her head vigorously as if to free her brain from a viral attack.

"Rob," Becky said softly towards the figure slumped lifelessly on the sofa.

"Rob," Becky said again, this time with a bit more volume, feeling a twinge of anxiety mixed with annoyance.

"ROB!" she finally yelled.

"What?" Rob muttered slowly inching his head in her direction.

Vigorously stabbing her right forefinger at the telephone, Becky mouthed, "Chloeeee."

"Oh, right-o," said Rob as slowly rising from the cushions, he wandered towards Becky keeping his gaze locked onto the television screen.

"Rob's here now, Chloe," said Becky quickly, thrusting the telephone into Rob's flaccid hand.

Rob's fingers immediately tightened into a fierce grip; Becky could hear traces of Chloe's distraught voice at the other end.

The shrieking continued as Rob dumbly clutched the receiver, offering an occasional grunt or an 'Oh God!' 'Oh No!'

And then suddenly, although it seemed much later to Becky who had collapsed on the sofa by now where she was becoming drowsy with all the background noise, she shot bolt upright as Rob shouted very loudly, "JESUS! NO! Christ Chloe, you CAN'T mean that, he can't have, he just can't have. Oh God, I'm so so sorry".

"Look, Chloe, don't you worry, I'm coming. I'll go and pack now and be on the first train in the morning. What? Oh don't worry, it's OK, the kids just finished school. Becky? Yes, sure she'll manage, she'll cope, sort things out, so don't worry I'll be with you in the morning. Jesus, Chloe, what a terrible, dreadful shock. Look, I want you to get yourself a very large G&T and get to bed, OK? And just hang on in there, I'll be with you in a few hours. OK? Now ring me any time, even if it's 3 a.m. Just hang on, Chloe, I'm on my way."

Becky could hear Chloe sobbing as Rob hung up.

"Jesus!" he said again loudly.

Polly and Wills momentarily distracted by the unusual sound of their father's voice, looked up as Rob came back into the room.

"Daddy?" they said loudly, in unison. But little expectant worried faces were met with a stern glare as Rob slammed out of the sitting room and stomped up the stairs.

The children solemnly shrugged at Becky before returning their attention to the television screen.

Becky slowly rose from the sofa, before making her way upstairs after Rob.

In their bedroom, she found clothes all over the floor, a large suitcase on the bed, and Rob galvanised in manic action such as she had never seen before.

Becky stood silently watching for a moment or two before speaking Rob's name gently.

"Rob, darling, what's going on?"

"Uh?" Rob said, not bothering to look up as he emptied the entire contents of his sock drawer onto the floor.

"Rob, look at me!" Becky said, a little louder this time. "What is it?"

"Look, why don't you just leave me to it?" Rob said sharply, glaring at Becky momentarily.

"Rob! what has happened to Chloe?" Becky yelled at last, at the top of her voice.

"Hugh is dead. Alright? D-E-A-D!" he yelled back at Becky.

"WHAT?" Becky shrieked, "What do you mean dead?"

Stopping his frenzied packing, Rob stood up straight and facing Becky said in a firm voice…

God, he's like a complete stranger, Becky thought, *I don't know who this man is any more.*

"Hugh died. In hospital. An hour ago. Massive heart attack. Chloe needs me. So I am going to her. End of story."

And with that, Rob resumed his packing activities, oblivious to Becky standing in their bedroom door tears streaming down her face.

"But, what about us, what about the children? You can't just go and leave us. You're not well, Rob. How can you look after Chloe if you're not well? What about your parents, your sister, your brother, they're all so much nearer, practically next door …"

But her words may as well have fallen on deaf ears. Rob did not reply, and with Becky still watching and waiting in a state of shock from the bedroom door, he proceeded to fasten his suitcase, undress and get into bed, only murmuring before turning out the bedside light, "I'm leaving at 10. Make sure you're up." And with that darkness fell upon the room.

Backing out slowly, Becky shut the bedroom door behind her quietly before sliding down onto the floor, thrusting her hands over her face and sobbing silently into the abyss in front of her.

* * *

The alarm woke Becky at 7; struggling out of a heavy and for once dreamless sleep, she fell out of bed and crawled towards the bathroom. Becky quickly came to when she found her way barred by a locked door; splashing and humming noises shocked her wide awake. Turning her head sharply, she saw to her amazement that the bed was completely empty. Slowly, she rotated her head back in the direction of the bathroom door; with a sharp intake of breath it suddenly dawned on her that Rob was up, awake and was first in the bathroom. This had not happened for years. About to bang her fists in frustration on the firmly shut door, Becky gave up and rising to her feet stumbled out of the bedroom before heading downstairs to the kitchen.

She made herself a cup of tea with a mountain of sugar before flinging on outdoor gear over her pyjamas and calling to the dogs. Becky stomped out into a beautiful spring morning, and suddenly the world and all her worries evaporated. After feeding the hens and letting out the rabbit, Becky sat for a while on the old bench under a blossoming apple tree. Bees hummed and birds sang as if fit to burst with joy in the soft morning air; for a few precious moments, Becky felt overwhelmed by a wonderful sense of peace and tranquillity.

Her reverie was abruptly shattered however by the sound of Rob's strident voice shouting her name out of the bathroom window.

"I'm here," Becky shouted wearily, getting up slowly and walking back towards the house, Flake and Cadbury bounding at her side.

"Where the helluv you been?" Rob yelled, his red face sticking out of the window.

Becky looked up at him without answering, before returning to the kitchen.

Laying out plates, cereal, a jug of milk and a bowl of sugar on the kitchen table, she warily glanced at the clock.

'Ten past eight. must go and wake the children, shower, ring Leo, sort breakfast, and get everyone into the car by ten past nine...' she quickly thought, struggling to swallow the panic that rose in her throat threatening to choke her.

'Rob's train is at ten past ten, and it's three-quarters of an hour to the station' ...

Galvanised by the activity agenda that had been somehow formulated in her brain without any apparent prior planning, Becky shot upstairs and into action.

Waking the children, she quickly showered and dressed, ignoring Rob's moans and complaints, before swiftly helping first William and then Polly to dress and hurrying them downstairs to breakfast; it felt like a normal school day. However, it was not.

Shovelling rice crispies into her mouth, Becky reflected that Leo would have to wait for an explanation until she arrived very late for work.

'I'll take the children to work and sort Leo out when I get there ...'

Becky, Rob, Polly, Wills, Flake and Cadbury piled silently into the little car, the children and dogs crammed into the back. The earlier spring sunshine gave way to driving rain as they set off ponderously for Chellingford Railway Station.

"Well, I hope ..." trailed Becky into the clammy atmosphere.

"What?" Rob retorted sharply.

"Nothing," said Becky quietly, concentrating hard on maintaining equilibrium in the overloaded car.

"Dad!" said Polly loudly into Rob's left ear. "My birthday's very soon!"

"You won't forget, will you?" she added wistfully.

"No Polly, no," replied Rob quietly, keeping his gaze fixed on the road ahead. "I'll be home by then."

"Will you?" Polly said brightly, and turning to William, she reeled off a list of birthday wishes in a loud voice that made Becky wince.

"Daddy home; Mummy happy; Wills quiet and behaving hisself; Polly with lots of lovely presents and lots of balloons; a great, big 'normous chocklick cake with a pink teddy and pink candles on top, and white rabbit at my Bouncy Castle Party!" she ended very loudly.

"Well Polly, that's quite a list!" shouted Becky from the driving seat, "better send it off pronto to the birthday fairy so she can get cracking!"

"Y E E E S S!" shrieked Polly, and William started bouncing up and down on his seat between Flake and Cadbury.

"QUIET! all of you!" shouted Rob, "this is no time for fun."

"That's where you're wrong," retorted Becky suddenly stung by his meanness.

"Keep your eyes on the road woman," yelled Rob as the overloaded car swerved perilously under a canopy of dripping trees.

They continued in silence except for the nervous panting of the dogs, air hungry and stressed by being in such close proximity to domestic unrest.

"Well, here we are, just in time for your train!" shouted Becky breathlessly as disengaging the gears and slamming on the brakes she ground the car to a halt scattering gravel and jerking everyone's heads sharply forwards.

"OK, everyone out!"

"Yeah!" shouted the children.

"Train's coming!" shrieked Wills loudly into Rob's right ear.

"Quick, quick Daddy, you'll miss it!" squealed Polly urgently.

"That's the down train Polly," replied Rob pompously. "The London train arrives in three minutes on the other side of the bridge."

"Hurry, hurry, Daddy, quick it's coming, I can see lights flashing."

"Please let us out," yelled Polly and William in unison.

"No, it's alright, you two stay here with Mum and the dogs. Anyway it's wet outside," said Rob firmly.

He hasn't spoken like this for months and months, thought Becky, watching her husband silently. *I have the distinct feeling he's relieved to be going.*

Still puzzling over Rob's transformation and hurt by his cool, detached attitude towards her, Becky spoke out loud: "Yes darlings, Daddy's right. Give him a big hug and a kiss and we'll wave to the train from the car."

"Right, I'm off then," said Rob abruptly, turning to give Becky a peck on the cheek.

I wonder if he's feeling guilty, Becky suddenly thought. *Maybe that's why he's so off with me; yes, that must be it.*

"Bye darlings, I'll see you very soon, we'll talk lots on the phone, and I'll give your love to Aunty Chloe, OK?" Rob said backing rapidly out of the car and sticking his head towards Polly and William for a kiss. Flake and Cadbury however got there first and the children lost out as Rob slammed shut the car door, shouting, "Must hurry. Bye." And picking up his holdall, he pelted towards the railway bridge and up the steps two at a time as the London train drew into the station.

Becky watched this unusual display of sudden athleticism with growing disquiet.

The car was abnormally silent as they drove away at the same time as the departing train, but gradually the sniffs and gulps grew louder until both children were wailing. And of course the dogs followed suit.

And so it was that as Becky mindlessly changed from third down to fourth gear, she had a sudden vision of the dream she'd had in the depths of winter and once again experienced the fear she'd felt when adrift and alone in a little boat on a heaving sea about to be dashed onto the rocks. Except, she remembered, there was a stranger in the boat; well, it certainly wasn't Rob because he'd just buggered off.

Snapping out of her strange reverie, Becky turned on the CD player and selecting Vivaldi's Rites of Spring turned the volume up to maximum, thus drowning the cacophony arising from the back seat. Peace soon descended as the beautiful music floated around them all.

The car slowed as they entered the little woodland village of Hurstmere and Becky leaned over to turn down the music.

"Mummy?" Polly asked in an exaggerated whisper, amidst hiccoughs and a lot of noisy sniffing.

"Yes darling?" replied Becky concentrating on the busy road that wound through the village.

"I think Wills wet hithelf," she continued. Polly always lisped badly when either extremely excited or extremely anxious. "And Mummy, he'th gone to thleep with hith thumb in hith mouth."

"Don't worry darling," replied Becky gently, "we'll sort everything out when we get home."

Polly was asleep, also with a thumb in her mouth, when Becky drew up outside the house half an hour later.

* * *

"Becky! where the hell are you? It's 11 o'clock for Chrissake and the emails are mounting by the second," bellowed Leo down the line.

Becky was holding the receiver at least two feet from her left ear.

…"What's happened this time? Big toe got stuck in the plughole? … wouldn't be surprised at all, in fact nothing surprises me about you Becky, nothing at all, not a single little thing—gives me palpitations just wondering what's going to happen next!"

"Leo," said Becky firmly into the mouthpiece.

"…trouble is Becky, you're driving me bonkers, to bloody drink … *oh thank you darling, just what I need …*" Leo said in an aside to an obviously hovering Fizz, "Gin and bloody tonic at 11 a.m., bit bloody steep, but …"

"LEO !" shouted Becky.

"… did you actually speak?…" responded Leo rudely.

"I did Leo, and please would you let me explain—I need you to listen to me for just one minute, OK?" Becky said in a tone verging on desperation, tears hovering in the background.

"Eh? What? Yes, well, yes please do speak, go ahead, I'm just going to sit down," barked Leo, albeit in a quieter tone.

"The thing is, Leo," began Becky, biting her lip hard to stop herself from bursting into tears. "The thing is, that Rob's gone up to London…"

"Gone up to London, so what?" Leo snarled.

The tears that had been welling up, burst out as Becky continued in sobs, "But he's only 41, Leo, only 41, that's so young…"

"Stop blubbing, woman, you're not making sense one bit," he snapped.

"But Rob's sister's husband dropped down dead yesterday!" Becky finally yelled.

"What did you say?" Leo said, before quickly adding, "No, on second thoughts, forget I said that. Just take a deep breath and tell me what's going on Becky."

By this time Becky was crying inconsolably. Seconds later, a very large, loud sniff resounded in Leo's ear making him wince. Holding the receiver a few inches away, he exhaled loudly puffing out both his cheeks in the process before inhaling deeply.

"Becky," said Leo quite gently for him, "what is the matter? Do tell me."

"Only 41 Leo, only 41…" Becky whispered, then loudly and rapidly "…how unfair is that?"

"Hrmph, yes Becky," replied Leo, much calmer now, the gin having worked its magic on his shoulder and jaw muscles. "Er, yes, definitely …"

Becky sniffed loudly down the phone.

"That's bloody tragic!" Leo suddenly shouted.

"Leo!" shouted Becky back, "that's the reason why I'm not at work!"

"But my husband left," Becky continued jerkily, "which is fair enough in the terrible circumstances, but the point I am making, Leo, the point I am making is that when he left, he was not ill! What does that say to you, Leo? What does that tell you, Leo? My husband became 'normal' as soon as he spoke to his sister and she told him what had happened!" she finished, shouting.

"Erm, yes, Becky, I think I see where you're coming from," stuttered Leo. "Er, look, take the rest of the day off, OK? I'll cope, Fizz'll help, won't you, darling?"

In the background, Becky thought she heard Fizz sighing deeply and loudly, or maybe she was mistaken in her current wild state?

"Right, OK, yes thanks, Leo. Thank you very much. That would be such a great help, if you really don't mind that is. And I'll see you in the morning," Becky rambled on.

"But Leo!", she continued loudly, "It would be OK, wouldn't it, if I brought the kids with me?"

"The thing is," she added rapidly, feeling that if she didn't now say what she was going to say all would be lost, job and family up the creek without a paddle. "Thing is Leo," Becky repeated, "I've no one now to look after them, now that Rob's not here, it's school holidays, and there's no one else, you see," she finished bleakly.

Christ! thought Leo, this *woman's a wild card, a bloody liability if I was being honest with myself. I picked a right one here. Only way is to go with the flow, hate that expression, go with the flow like wine out of a bottle. Christ Almighty, add Pierre to the soup, and hey presto whadawe have? Yeah, we have hot soup, explosion, eruption.*

"Leo? Are you still there?" Becky said, almost normally.

"Jesus," he concluded, loudly and vocally, "yeah, yes, of course, whatever, just so long as the work gets done, OK?"

At that, the line went dead, leaving Becky staring open-mouthed at the receiver that now emitted the 'death tone,' *like the machines on hospital TV programmes,* she mused solemnly, *that go monotone the minute someone dies.*

Hope Leo hasn't dropped dead too, thought Becky momentarily before swiftly jerking herself back to conscious time ... children dozing on the sofa oblivious of the Leo phone call, house in chaos, job in chaos, marriage in chaos, life in chaos.

The next morning, however, bright and early, Becky, Polly, Wills, Flake and Cadbury, all piled into the car and set off to 'work.'

"Morning, all!" boomed Leo from the top floor, "Come on up!"

"Hello, Leo," said Becky, quite formally for she was really rather nervous.

"You know Flake and Cadbury, of course," she continued in a singsong voice.

Leo raised an eyebrow.

"Now, may I introduce you to Polly who is seven and a half years old, and William who is six?"

Both children stared open-mouthed at the very large person blocking the doorway to the office beyond.

Flake and Cadbury banged tails loudly, setting up a symphony on the banisters.

"Hrmm," Leo cleared his throat, "in you come, all of you, make yourselves at home! Plenty of paper and pencils on the floor down there, see, Fizz thought you'd like it down there," he continued pointing to Flake and Cadbury's appointed space under Becky's desk.

All four made a bee-line for safety, as Becky stood face to face with Leo.

"Right now, Becky," said Leo gruffly, clearing his throat. "Onwards and upwards as they say, get on with it, there's a mountain waiting on your desk. I'm just off downstairs for a moment, leave you to it, I'll be back with coffee and whatever in a bit."

Becky slumped into her chair before peeping under her desk to check that what she thought was there was not entirely of her imagination. It was not. Wills, Polly, Flake and Cadbury all had their tongues lolling out of their mouths—the children drawing with intense concentration, the dogs merely drooling in anticipation of elevenses and biscuits.

"OK, here goes," thought Becky, silently sending a prayer into the ether in desperate hope that it would be heard and answered, and that the day would pass without mishap.

Five minutes later, as Becky at last relaxed into 'concentrating-on-work' mode, a sudden shriek from Polly sent her teeth slamming into her tongue, causing several puncture wounds.

"What, Pol, what!? Are you alright?" Becky lisped, bending down to look at the underground scene.

"Oh 'snothing, Mum," sang Polly, "I was just really 'cited by my picture! Look!" she shrieked thrusting a piece of paper under Becky's nose; gradual visual adjustment showed Becky that outside what looked like a house of sorts on fire, with spiky 'flames' appearing all over the page, were stick people, four to be exact.

"Oh thaths really good, Pol," lisped Becky again painfully.

"Darling, pleath be ath quiet ath a mouth, Mummyth got lotth of work to do, and Leo will be back thoon! Tho Thhhh!!"

"OK!" was the whispered reply.

"They've been extraordinarily good, your brood, Becky," observed Leo later, feet on his desk, tapping his mouth with a pen.

"Why don't you all head off home now? It's well after 2, and we've caught up on most of the backlog, urgent stuff's all dealt with so why don't you just 'take off,' have tomorrow off to get yourself sorted. Gimme a ring in the morning when you've peace and quiet and we'll make plans," he added with a knowing glint in his eye.

Becky regarded him suspiciously before gathering together her by now drowsy family and heading off towards the office door.

"Thanks, Leo," said Becky seriously, turning back to look at him fair and square in the eyes. She was genuinely and overwhelmingly grateful.

"That's OK, chicken," he replied, looking up at her kindly, "just look after yourself and that brood of yours. See you in a couple of days, and thanks for coming in by the way."

With that, he turned abruptly to the handset and picking it up began rapidly dialling a long number.

Becky turned her head slightly to the right, cocking her left ear to listen. Two floors down and she just caught, "Ah, Pierre mon ami …" then, the office door suddenly slammed shut. Becky sighed deeply before she and the children and the dogs descended to the ground floor and out to the waiting car.

June

Rob relaxed on an elegant chaiselongue that graced the luxurious drawing room of Chloe's Richmond mansion. French doors from the drawing room led outdoors onto the secluded garden at the back of the beautiful house. The huge open-plan space on the ground floor encompassed, at the opposite end to the garden, a massive, ultra-modern kitchen; an exquisite dining area lay between kitchen and drawing room. This was a house of massive and perfect proportions. Rob felt comfortable, relaxed, and at home, despite the emotional tragedies surrounding him.

"I say, Chlo', that was a superb evening. You've some really great friends, you know, and how supportive they are," Rob mused, a hint of envy trickling out, unnoticed by a preoccupied Chloe stacking crystal glasses and Meissen china in the dishwasher.

"Mind you," he continued sagely, "you so deserve loads of love and support. And surely after all you've been through, you deserve to sit back and relax a bit, go out to the movies, have dinner out. I'll be here, I'll support you."

"Yes," replied Chloe faintly from the kitchen. Across the broad expansive space between them, Chloe continued in a slightly more confident voice, "I'm certainly blessed with my wonderful friends. My wonderful brother too," she added, turning her gaze across the Venetian floor tiles across the space to her brother's flushed and beaming face.

"I can't tell you how much it means to me to be here for you, Chloe," replied Rob, tears glistening in his dark hazel eyes. "I couldn't bear being away from you knowing you were on your own and suffering, in so much pain …" he finished, turning his face away to cast his gaze into the shadows of the garden beyond.

"Rob," said Chloe, her voice quivering with emotion, "I can't begin to tell you what it has meant to me, you being here—you have been, and are, my rock, my life support system; without you I couldn't have survived the last few weeks."

"But I worry so much about you," she continued earnestly. "Becky, your beautiful children, all you've left behind. And no please Rob, don't interrupt. And all for me, your sister. I am so very touched and so deeply grateful—you'll never know just how much. But—no please Rob, let me finish—I think I can really manage now, on my own. I need to get back to work and—what? What did you just say?"

"I said, Chloe," replied Rob, "I said," he repeated emphatically, "I'm staying! Isn't it great? I just heard today I've got a job—a job Chloe! The first time in God knows how long, and it's here, in London, Whitcomb Street to be precise, an ad agency—you know, sort of general admin, making sure everything runs smoothly! And Chloe, I love it there, it feels so right!"

"But Rob," stammered Chloe, "what about…"

"Don't ask, Chloe, don't even go there, it's not a problem, I promise. If they want to see me and be with me, then they can jolly well move on up here, can't they? I mean, what's the problem, where's the hitch? Sell that draughty old barn of a place, rehouse les animals, and hey presto! Problem solved! Plus," Rob added gleefully, "I'll be back as main breadwinner; Becky can get herself another job, and Polls and William? Well, they're just bound to love going to school up here—imagine, school in London? They'd fit in anywhere those two! So you see Chloe, it's all going to be alright, just fine; I've been thinking and planning and, my goodness, it's going to work, and work out really well; and we'll all be here for each other, no one feeling lost and lonely!"

"Rob, I, er, don't really know what to say!" stammered a clearly surprised Chloe. "That's quite an idea, and, my goodness, you've gone and got yourself a job! Why, Rob, that is amazing, I'm so pleased and happy for you! What do Becky and the children think? I'll bet they're absolutely thrilled to bits!" she continued handing Rob a large Laphroag whilst motioning for him to sit in Hugh's old chair.

"…er, they don't know yet, Chloe," replied Rob sinking into the deep soft leather chair whilst taking a long slow sip of the single malt, a blank expression appearing on his recently animated face.

"…what on earth do you mean Becky doesn't know yet?" Chloe replied sharply, standing by the huge fireplace, her face parallel to a large portrait photograph of her recently departed husband. "You must surely have talked it over with her before accepting the job?"

"No, I haven't actually," said Rob coldly. "Why should I? She's so busy down at her wine merchants and walking the dogs, she wouldn't even know if I became an astronaut and went to the moon and back."

"But what about Polly and William?" Chloe persisted, "Surely you've said something about it to them? After all, they'll need to be thinking about moving homes and schools, which is a lot to take on board at their age."

Rob's blank stare and reply answered her queries, and ignoring his sister's pleas on his family's behalf, he continued pompously.

"Now, Chlo' I don't want you worrying about these trivial matters, they are easily sortable, believe me! The main thing is I have a J-O-B! and You are not going to be alone!"

With that, Rob drained his glass, rose from Hugh's seat, and bent down to kiss his sister goodnight on the top of her head, before taking the stairs two at a time and disappearing like a puff of smoke into his large and luxurious bedroom with ensuite bathroom and large screen television.

"Well, well, well," mused Chloe to herself, before she too drained her glass and ascended the elegant staircase rather more slowly than her brother, and walked along the wide landing towards her own extravagant bedroom at the end of the long corridor.

* * *

Immaculately turned out in cream slacks and a French-style navy and cream striped top, Chloe kissed her brother's forehead good morning as she placed the large Spode teacup and saucer on the table beside the comfortable bed where Rob lay sleeping peacefully.

As Chloe headed back towards the bedroom door, she heard a sniffing sound followed by a murmur, "Versace, Divine! Divine, darling!... Are you off somewhere intriguing?" He continued, his left eye opening just a fraction.

"Go back to sleep for a while, darling," Chloe murmured. "The solicitor's due any moment now!" And she swiftly moved towards and out of the bedroom door, blowing Rob a kiss on the way out.

Rob continued to doze for a few seconds longer before his eyes sprang open; he was wide awake and thinking. Balancing elegant teacup on elegant saucer, Rob leant back against the soft, fluffy pillows to ponder his situation. All was going very well indeed he concluded 15 minutes later. Thirty minutes later as he soaked in a luxurious and deliciously scented foam bath, he considered and planned the next stage of his 'Rescue Rob,' or rather 'Rescue Rob and Chloe' plan.

Around about 10 o'clock, Rob entered the drawing room to find Chloe sitting at her antique bureau writing.

"Hi!" he said loudly and brightly. She looked up briefly and smiled at Rob before continuing with her writing.

"Busy?" Rob enquired. "Good meeting?" he continued, helping himself to a cup of filtered ground coffee, ignoring his sister's body language that she obviously did not want to be disturbed.

"Sorry?" Chloe looked up again, smiling perhaps a shade less brightly this time.

Rob glared at her over the rim of his coffee cup.

"Just wondering how your meeting went," he said, emphasising the word meeting, teeth set in an expression of veiled aggression. The Rottweiler of their childhood would have been proud of him.

"Fine thanks, why?" Chloe replied lightly, returning to her writing. She had not turned to look at her brother this time.

"Oh, nothing," said Rob, putting his cup and saucer down with a clatter before exiting the large comfortable room.

But Chloe's mood was shattered, and sighing deeply she rose and made her way slowly towards the conservatory at the back of the house where she knew her brother would be waiting, and sulking.

Isn't life strange, very odd somehow? she mused as she slowly made her way through the large kitchen towards the conservatory and the garden beyond. *...and it's so scary, totally unnerving that one moment here I am, in this house, blissfully happy and then all of a sudden like a bolt out of the blue, BANG, Hugh falls down dead, just disappears, vanishes ...my darling Hugh...and then straight away, before I know where I am and what has happened, this bizarre situation arises—my brother here, living with me, when for so many years he's been totally absent from my life—all of a sudden he's here and it's like he's trying to organise me, seeking to control everything in my life.*

Well, a grieving widow I may be but that does not mean I am helpless—no, far from it, he's forgotten just how tough I can be, he's forgotten I am older than him. But I'm really worried about his attitude towards Becky... if they did come to London, where would they all live?... as much as I love them, they're family, but there's no way they're coming to live here, I don't want it, Hugh would definitely have not allowed it... they'll just have to find their own place ... I'll talk to Rob now, before it's too late, before he's talked about it all to Becky ... But what I don't understand is that they've such a lovely old house, and there's the village school, and of course all those animals—dogs, cats, rabbits, hens, and God knows what else ...they have so much down there, the perfect place to raise a young family, not London after all that ... if we'd been able to have children, we would definitely have moved to the country, it's the only place, Hugh would have commuted...

But there Chloe's reverie ended. As she entered the conservatory, with its doors opening out onto the exquisitely planted but small garden beyond, she was met with a large sob and turning her head towards the direction of the sniffing and snivelling, her heart melted to see her brother completely crumpled and helpless, sitting on a wicker stool in the far corner.

"Chloe," Rob croaked, "I'm sorry, I should have told you everything before"

Sniffing loudly, he continued in a stronger, more determined tone, "Truth is old thing, me and Becky, well, we just don't rock together any more...haven't done for a long time in fact...nothing, not a squeak since William arrived, no sex, no love, no nothing, she just lives for those kids, and all those bloody animals...completely ignores me most of the time," he continued, his voice getting stronger, warming to his subject. "Well, what could I do when she bloody did it all, she left me out of everything, the kids don't notice I'm there half the time, just run bloody wild all over the place, and I can't stand it anymore, Chlo', I just can't take it. She doesn't care a toss, flouncing in from that job of hers with some posh sounding bottle of plonk every day, and it's Leo this and Leo that, and that's it, I've had enough of her…"

The beautiful early summer's day outside shimmered, it was perfect weather, and for once it seemed that the Wimbledon fortnight about to begin was to be blessed with endless sunshine. Chloe and Hugh had always been, Centre Court tickets were part of the annual agenda. It was one of Chloe's most favourite times of the year, and all of a sudden memories came flooding back … picnics in the park, opera under candlelight in the open air, Henley regatta, and their favourite, Wimbledon. But the stoicism that was Chloe's inheritance from their imperious mother won the day; she did not weep with her brother as he bathed in self-pity and denial, she stood firm and in control.

"Robert, if you don't mind, I have urgent matters to attend to that have been delayed enough today already. Now, listen to me, and don't interrupt, please. I do not wish to enter into the boiling pot that is your marriage to Becky, that is your affair, and whilst I sympathise with any difficulties you may have, I will not, I repeat I will not be a party to any of your bickering; I simply do not want to know as I am not in the right place to listen at the moment, I do not want to listen at the moment, I have just lost my husband, and I will not have you here under my roof contaminating my private space with your personal problems.

"They can wait and as far as I am concerned you have a choice, either you go back to your home and get yourself and your family together again or you remain in my home for as long as I deem fit, and whilst here you will conduct yourself in a respectable manner, you will go to your work that you seem to be so delighted about, and whilst you are in my house, you will behave respectfully and with maturity.

"Why don't you start thinking about setting a good, strong example to those lovely children of yours instead of bleating about the fact that they take no notice of you—of course they don't, if you don't interact with them, if you don't set them an example, a role model for them to look up to and respect? Now enough, I have said all I want to say, except to emphasise for once and for all, please Robert, would you start thinking about other people and not always and forever about yourself? I suggest, as a starting point, that you contact Becky and tell her what is going on, that you have a job up here, and then let her decide what she and the children would like to do in the circumstances; after all, I am sure that neither of you would truthfully want your precious children to be unhappy and in an environment where they could struggle and lose their way."

"Go out for a walk, Rob, across the Common, or just up and down the road, but get out of this house now before I throw you out, which I do not want to do but which I will if you do not get on, get your life in gear, and start thinking of people other than yourself, especially your family!"

July

The house was in a dilapidated sort of order, but order no less as Becky picked up the phone in the kitchen and dialled Leo's number.

"Leo?" Becky said, calmly and quite quietly.

"What? Who?" Leo yelled, "Who's that?"

"It's me, Becky!" she yelled back instantly shattering the carefully created calm atmosphere. The dogs barked and the children wailed. Becky groaned.

"Hold on a moment, Leo," she shouted, "I'll ring you back from upstairs."

Slamming down the receiver, Becky flew into the sitting room to check on Polly and William before bounding up the stairs two at a time.

"Leo! It's Becky again!" she said very loudly.

"No need to shout," replied a disgruntled voice.

"Sorry," Becky replied apologetically, "I'm here now! And Leo, I'm so sorry about all this—but there's only a couple of weeks now before the end of term and then things will get a bit…"

"Shut up for a minute, Becky, will you? I've got something to tell you so don't interrupt, just listen."

This is it thought Becky desperately. *I'm fired. Jobless. Husbandless. Penniless.*

"Spoke to Pierre yesterday," began Leo.

Ah, mused Becky, *I remember now, just as we were leaving work…*

"You still there, woman? Line's gone completely dead your end," continued Leo impatiently.

"No, I mean yes, Leo, I'm here, and I'm listening," replied Becky.

"Thank Christ for that, thought you'd bottled out on me; no pun intended!" shouted Leo, before giving a hoot of laughter at his own poor joke. Becky remained silent the other end.

"Oh alright then," he said peevishly, before continuing in a more serious tone. "Now, Becky, hope you don't mind but I told him about you and your problems, you know you being left on your own, two kids etc. etc., husband buggered off for God knows how long—do you know by the way what the score is there? No? well never mind, here's the plan…you have to get your life together, yes?"

"Well, yes, I do actually,, Leo," replied Becky seriously.

"Well, good, good, good! Now, as I was saying, here's the plan. Brilliant if I may say so; partly my idea, partly Pierre's! And the long and the short of it is that we need you to carry out a role reversal!"

"Sorry?" Becky squeaked, "A what?"

"Eh? Becky, for goodness sake, a role reversal," repeated Leo rolling the R's with dramatic aplomb.

"Leo, I'm sorry I just don't get your drift at all," replied Becky, her fragile mental processes working overtime as images flashed in front of her—Pierre dressed up as a waitress, herself as a butler. "This has gone far enough," she told herself, "time to give in the notice and sign up for benefit."

"Leo, I…" began Becky, but a loud bark at the other end of the receiver prevented her speaking further.

"Just clearing my throat," growled Leo, "now, just be quiet for one moment, would you, please!"

"O…" croaked Becky.

"Not a squeak!" yelled Leo impatiently.

"Now. At the end of the summer term, which I assume is any day now," he continued more calmly as he warmed to his subject, "I want you to put your chickens, ducks, dogs, rabbits or whatever else you have into care—yes, temporarily of course…" he added with a touch of sarcasm in response to a gasp from Becky. "You and your children will then 'allez en France', and by that I mean buzz off to France for the summer, stay at Pierre's place, he's got maids and whatnot, and whilst your kiddies have fun—Pierre's got a couple of sprogs too—you, Becky," continued Leo, saying her name with emphasis as if, Becky felt, she were destined for a visit to Madame La Guillotine. "You carry on working! Point is I need you to do some R&D for me, research and development that is, savie? Have a look around, get the feel of the place, go visit the vineyards near Pierre's pad, taste some wines, look out for new ones—you've got a good 'nose' Becky; also I'm sure you're a damned good cook, so you may have a better idea than either Pierre or myself what new wines we could introduce that go well with English cuisine, see what I mean? get my drift? No, don't answer yet, please."

"Now just so as you're completely in the picture," Leo continued, "Pierre is, or rather was until recently, a married man, and as I said has two smalls of his own—boy and a girl, eight and five, I think. Maids, nannies or whatever are about so you can relax, work, and get rid of that scatty behaviour! And do me and the business a huge favour into the bargain! What do you think of that?" He finished expansively. "Gets you out of my hair for a few weeks!" he muttered aside.

"What did you say, Leo?" Becky said sharply.

"Me? Nothing, nothing at all. Now, what's it to be then girl? Gift on a plate or misery in a pancake?"

"I don't see what pancakes have to do with all this, Leo," replied Becky feistily; she was feeling piqued as well as extremely scared.

"What? Pancakes? What the hell are you going on about? Is it on or not? Are you going or staying? Choice is quite simple really. Tell me tomorrow. Sleep on it."

And with that, the line went dead.

"Christmas night!" pondered Becky, slumping into her favourite chair by the Aga where a bean casserole slowly and aromatically simmered. All the doors and windows were open, and Becky could just make out eight upwardly pointing and wiggling paws; Maurice sat on the window sill observing with barely concealed disdain. Having been indoors most of the day in front of the television, Polly and William were now shrieking and screaming outside, running around stark-naked pretending to be alien aeroplanes!

"First and foremost, a glass of wine is definitely called for!" sighed Becky, as she eased the cork out of a Cotes de Ventoux red that Leo had thrust upon her yesterday. Pouring the sunburnt liquid into a glass, Becky returned to her chair to continue her reverie, feet curled under her.

Help! yes, but hey, what an actually fantastic idea— Polly and Wills get to have a long summer break away from 'it all' and they'll be looked after and have playmates; I get to go away and work, so the pennies come in and we have a long holiday as well! Oh, and I know...perhaps Mum and Dad may like a break—then they could come here... Becky's thoughts continued, and she felt a rising enthusiasm as a plan gradually took shape, *...enjoy the house and the garden, at the same time as keeping an eye on the animals ... Wow! This really could be the answer, well to the summer holidays at least!*

June had already bloomed into July and the end of the summer term and the school year loomed on the horizon. Both children had struggled this term; Polly had become steadily quieter whilst William had become naughtier, and if possible, noisier. Poor Miss Clasby looked a shadow of her former self; headmaster merely scowled at everyone, and he never spoke, not to anyone at all.

"Mum! Hello! It's me, Becky! Yes, we're OK thanks, just exhausted that's all and looking forward to the end of term! No, no word from Rob ... no, not a thing now for a couple of weeks ... no, I know Mum, it's actually six weeks since he was last home for the weekend ... yes, I know Mum, it was a disaster I agree ...Anyway, if you've got five minutes and can talk now, I've something I want to put to you and Dad!" Becky carried on brightly.

"Well!" her mother said, when Becky had finished explaining her plan, "Now that does sound like a good idea, and I know that it would do your father such a lot of good, get his mind off all his aches and pains, and you know how much he loves the animals, and how much I love pottering in your garden! Why on earth not? Just give me ten minutes to have a word with Dad, and I'll ring you straight back. Love you, darling, bye!"

Tears flooding her eyes, Becky poured herself another glass of Leo's red wine, and breathing out loudly, cheeks ballooning under the pressure, sent a silent but alcoholic 'let my plan work' plea into the ether.

Five minutes later, Becky shot out of the chair, flinging Cotes du Ventoux all over the kitchen floor, as the telephone rang with what felt like extreme urgency.

"Darling, it's me! Mum! Yes, darling, we'd love to come. Yes, everything's fine, I'm so excited!"

"Oh, so am I, Mum, that's just wonderful, thank you both so much!" exclaimed Becky excitedly. "How soon before you can come—it would be so lovely if we could spend a few days together before we have to leave for France?"

"Leave it with me, darling!" replied Becky's mother. "When do you plan to be off? What? About the 25th of July? OK, I'll see if we can come a few days before you go … but I'll have to check with your father, you know what he's like with the garden! It'll do him such a lot of good to get away for a bit!"

August

Becky breathed in deeply, revelling in the mingled and exquisitely aromatic and exotic scents of jasmine, santolina, thyme, and lavender that wafted around her on the warm air. She closed her eyes and raised her pale face to the sun. Breathing out slowly, she finally relaxed, allowing the afterglow of the simple but delicious lunch to wash over her—salade Nicoise dripping olive oil and garlic, chunks of fresh baguette, soft, creamy and nutty Banon cheese, numerous glasses of a perfectly chilled white Chateauneuf-du-Pape. Cicadas gently thrummed.

I've died and gone to heaven was the last thought Becky had as she drifted into a blissful, relaxing sleep. She dreamed she was following a dark handsome man through a field of wavering corn; they were running; suddenly he turned, and holding out his arms towards her, swept her into a passionate embrace…a scream nearby assaulted her senses, she became confused, and the cornfield retreated at warp speed; her eyes bolted open like wagon wheels, and she felt her heart thundering like a herd of wild horses in flight.

Becky shot to her feet; however, fear was replaced by overwhelming relief as she focused on Polly sitting at the base of a small water slide, her face a picture of ecstasy.

Wills emitted an equally piercing yell as he slid down head first, followed by Patrick-Antoine and finally little Francelle. Dark and blond heads mingled together, bobbing around the shallow pool at the base of the mini-slide.

Becky gradually became aware of firm but very gentle pressure being applied to her left shoulder; she stopped breathing altogether as out of the corner of her eye, she spied Pierre's tanned, well-manicured hand. The hand remained where it was until Becky had relaxed back into her chair and started breathing again, inhaling as she did the unusual and lemony fragrance of his aftershave.

Oh my God! thought Becky, *I wish he'd put his hand right back again where it was, that was amazing, just like an electric shock, only a lovely one!*

"You should try to relax more, Becki, you are safe 'erre," said Pierre gently, settling himself back into his chair next to hers, and smiling at her; his sexy French voice seemed to caress her name.

Becky responded by turning her head slowly towards Pierre until their eyes met; she allowed a slow and she hoped seductive smile to spread across her lips; an unfamiliar but delicious sensation flooded her nether regions.

Just as Becky reached out to touch Pierre's hand, now resting passively on the arm of his chair, he stood up suddenly, knocking the chair over in the process. Becky shot a startled look in his direction; his eyes held hers for a second, before muttering in French "Excuse-moi un moment. il faut cherche le café"; and with that, Pierre turned abruptly and walked rapidly back towards the house.

"Am I dreaming?" Becky mused, once more relaxed and sipping her wine.

Gazing into the distance as at an exquisitely beautiful painting, her eyes slowly focused on the perfect Provencal landscape, and she allowed herself the luxury of an exquisitely delicious thought; *I think Pierre went a trifle pink under that gorgeous tan of his. Now, why would that be I wonder? I certainly felt something, that spark when he touched me...I think he felt it too, and I think he's embarrassed!*

Becky inhaled the seductively scented air as she languorously stretched her arms above her head; bringing her hands together at the nape of her neck, her head relaxed back and she let out a deep sigh of contentment.

A loud crash and the sound of tinkling pieces of china came from the courtyard followed by a very loud,

"Merd!"

"Marise! vien ici, vite, vite, vite!" Pierre shouted out.

…

19-year-old Marise, the home help, seemed to Becky to be a minor miracle. Every morning at around 6, she arrived on her bicycle from her parent's tiny vineyard 8km away, having stopped en route at the boulangerie in the little village of St Paul des Eglises. Into her bicycle basket, she packed a quantity of fragrant croissants for breakfast and various shapes and sizes of bread for the day.

On arrival at La Maison des Olivieres, Marise then proceeded to make lists for Pierre of any additional supplies that might be needed, before setting up breakfast on the terrace, putting milk to slowly warm on the large range, grinding beans for coffee, and setting the water on to boil.

She then went to wake the children, opening the shutters and setting out their clothes, before chivvying them into the bathroom as if herding cows in an alpine meadow, with a gentle, "Allee, allee," adding "Vite, vite," if necessary to anyone who lagged behind. Of course, since Becky, Polly and William's arrival, her little herd had expanded. Marise was a kind, gentle soul who adored Pierre's children and had immediately taken Becky's two under her wing; the pair had seemed to her like a couple of little orphans when they first arrived.

Not orphans now, thank goodness, thought Marise as she herded the four children back into the large, sunny bedroom where they all slept.

To Polly and William, it had been like arriving in a place like Wonderland when, asleep in the car at 4 a.m., having driven for what seemed like thousands of miles, they slowly became aware of the crunch of gravel and then the car becoming silent.

"Mummy, whath happning?" Polly had lisped anxiously, thumb in her mouth.

Wills had remained silent, yawning with eyes still shut tight.

"Polls, Wills, we've arrived!" Becky had whispered; sighing, stretching and then slowly opening the car door, she had stepped out onto the gravel and into the warm scented early morning air, gentle light only just beginning to kiss the horizon.

"Where's the swimming pool, Mum?" William had suddenly yelled.

Shooting back into the car and quickly but quietly closing the door, Becky had whispered vehemently, "Hush, Wills, hush, hush, hush darling, everyone's asleep, we don't want to wake them, do we?"

After five minutes, Polly had broken the silence by saying quite loudly, "Well, Mummy, hadn't they better get up and say hello?"

"Well, yes, darling, but we've arrived so much earlier than I said we would, I thought we'd be arriving around about early breakfast-time, not at very late bedtime! So, what we're going to do is go back to sleep, and wake up again when it's nice and light and proper morning, and breakfast time! OK?"

Becky, exhausted though she was by the long, long journey from Cherbourg, could not sleep; Polly and William however had swiftly returned to Neverland. It was an exquisite feeling; Becky had mused in her exhausted reverie:

We are here and we are safe. I don't know what happens next but we've done it and for a while, until I know what to do, we have a safe haven, somewhere to heal our wounds. Poor babies, my poor, poor darlings, so brave, and so very sensitive and vulnerable. How could he...? She began, and then had stopped. *But we are here now and this is the very beginning of a new and wonderful life!* And with that thought shimmering in her mind, Becky had fallen asleep, to be woken an hour later by Marise's gentle tapping on the car window in the soft early morning light.

* * *

"Er, cette apres midi, Becki, pardon, sorry, this afternoon Becky," said Pierre brusquely, "qu'est que vous faites? Er sorry, what are you going to do?"

"Sorry, Pierre, what was that? I didn't quite catch what you said?" Becky yawned, stretching out her limbs in front of her like a lazy lioness. *Well, I do believe he's blushing again under that tan,* she mused, fixing her gaze on Pierre's dark, liquid eyes. *God he's gorgeous,* was the next thought bubble that emitted from the top of Becky's dark curly head of hair.

Fixing his eyes on a point just above Becky's head, as if seeking to read her thought bubbles, Pierre replied curtly, "parce que, because, I 'ave to attend a meeting of vigneurs in St Paul Trois Chateaux." Then meeting her gaze directly, he continued, "You may come if you wish, it would impress Leo per'aps, and Marise, she will look after les enfants…"

"No, it's alright, Pierre, thank you, but not today, I just feel like relaxing completely, also I have some serious thinking to do. But another day, I would love to come with you, I'm sure there's an awful lot for me to learn."

Becky could have sworn Pierre's shoulders relaxed in relief response; he was clearly uneasy, perhaps the meeting would sweep all that under the carpet.

Pierre resolved to return without a trace of discomfort and in charge of his emotions once more. He was not a little annoyed to be thus affected by Becky as not so very long ago he had viewed her, on his last visit to England, as a walking disaster.

The tyres of his sleek, convertible, pale blue BMW sent fountains of gravel flying as Pierre sped off down the drive as if pursued by demons. Becky smiled to herself as she relaxed again on the sun-bed, lowering her sunglasses on to the bridge of her nose and raised her glass of chilled white wine to her lips.

Mm…Mercedes…BMW…what else is he hiding?… what a handsome dark horse…

The four children, by now lifelong allies, lay on their stomachs on a large rug spread out beneath the large, leafy branches of a gigantic black fig tree, reading. The occasional happy tinkle of laughter wafted across to Becky along with the warm throbbing and insistent sound of the cicadas.

* * *

The days turned into weeks, each one filled with laughter, and the most wonderful sense of freedom and relaxation spread through Becky's whole being as if she were constantly bathed in a sea of sunshine and happiness. She loved and felt totally at home in the beautiful Provencal region; it enveloped her in its timeless rhythm of life that stretched back over the centuries; it held for her a deep sense of beauty and security and peace such as she had never known; and Becky loved and respected the simplicity and the timelessness of the bread, the wine, the olives and their oil.

This is not real; this is not happening! Becky often mused, sometimes having to pinch herself hard so far removed had she become from all they had left behind. True, Leo was on the phone to either her or Pierre, or both, almost daily, but work such as it was, was a pleasure not a chore. Becky had been on many vineyard visits with Pierre where they had tasted the exquisite nectar of the region, laughing together at Becky's unusual 'nose'—she was highly imaginative and sometimes caught traces and whiffs of the most obscure substances such as coal, mango, and sherbet. Her knowledge grew as did her friendship with Pierre. Not since that long ago day shortly after they had first arrived, had Becky noticed anything uneasy about Pierre's behaviour. He was always outgoing, chatty, funny, in control; and he liked it that way.

Towards the middle of August, Becky's thoughts began to turn towards school and home and her parents, and of course, Rob. She had been in regular contact with her mother and father, and the children sometimes had chatty conversations with them, bubbling over with enthusiasm about the wonderful time they were having. All was well at home and her parents were thoroughly enjoying the garden, and also the animals, including the hens! Becky had tried to contact Rob at Chloe's house a few times, but always got the answer machine, and he never returned her calls. Polly and William rarely asked about their father, usually when they were tired. Only last week, when Becky had gone in to kiss the children goodnight, Polly with thumb in mouth lisped, "Why doethn't Daddy come to see us?" William just drifting off to sleep in the next bed, said drowsily "Cos he's busy, stupid."

"Wills, Polly's not stupid," Becky had said softly, "but you're right, Daddy is very busy, and I expect we'll see him very soon."

"I like it here," Polly had whispered.

"Me too," said Wills, and with that, they both fell instantly fast asleep.

Becky's evenings were peaceful and relaxed once the children slept. She and Pierre would sit outdoors on the patio under the stars, and over a late supper talked together about anything and everything, often sharing a bottle of a particularly favourite wine they had tasted that day. And on the few nights when Becky appeared distracted by her thoughts of home, Pierre would always notice and gently ease out of her what she was worrying about. By the end of the meal, she was always relaxed and happy again as if she had not a care in the world. And every night, she slept deeply, dreamlessly and peacefully.

Becky was occasionally able to open the door a crack or two onto Pierre's life, but he always clammed up and shut the door firmly if she happened to probe too deeply. It was obvious though that he too had been badly hurt, and all Becky knew was that his wife Chantelle had left him and the children for a wealthy businessman who lived on the Cote d'Azur and owned a very large gin palace; apparently, Chantelle's boyfriend had five children of his own who spent most of their time with their mother in Paris. Becky gleaned that although Pierre didn't say as much, Patrick-Antoine and Francelle rarely saw their mother.

* * *

The morning of departure dawned, hot and still, as if in suspense. It was the very last day of August.

Squeezing every little drop out of this wonderful place before facing the music... Becky mused as she and Pierre sat quietly outside, drinking coffee, whilst waiting for the children to join them.

"Eh bien mes enfants!" exclaimed Pierre cheerfully as Patrick-Antoine and Polly followed by Wills and Francelle shuffled towards the table, looking totally miserable. Pierre winked discreetly at Becky before leaning forwards and adding in a gentle voice, "Now, what is all this about? Why the long faces?"

Polly sniffed loudly, William hiccoughed, whilst Patrick-Antoine looked at the ground sullenly; Francelle's lower lip began to quiver.

"Hey, now, mes enfants!" continued Pierre, loudly and cheerfully, "What is this un'appiness? Why so sad? Why! Don't you know? It is not long before it is Christmas! Now is it?!" He finished in a flourish, beaming all over his face.

Becky's face too wore a big, warm smile.

The children slowly raised their eyes, suspiciously regarding Pierre and Becky's faces for a second or two, before simultaneously letting out whoops and shouts and shrieks of joy and excitement.

"Wow!" shrieked Polly and William in unison. "We're coming back for Christmas! Aren't we, aren't we…aren't we, Mum?" Polly finished, as all of a sudden her little lit-up face became serious, and a quiver started rippling along her bottom lip. Wills, Patrick-Antoine and Francelle all looked horrified as they too realised that 'it' may not all be going to happen after all…

"No, No, No, my angels!" cried Becky, "We really are coming back for Christmas, it's all true!"

"C'est vrai mes enfants! We will have Christmas all together!" said Pierre happily, before looking directly at Becky and adding, "just like one big 'appy family."

Becky held his gaze for a moment, before directing her eyes rapidly to the ground, blushing profusely.

A very loud 'Whoopeeeeeeeeee!' was the children's response.

With a big sigh and a large smile spreading all over her face, Becky turned first to Francelle, bending down to give her a hug, before turning to Patrick-Antoine to give him also a hug; finally, she turned towards Pierre, as heart thumping she allowed herself to be enveloped in his arms, where he held her tightly before kissing her tenderly on both cheeks, releasing her and swiftly turning to hug and shake hands with William and Polly who were standing next to Patrick-Antoine and Francelle watching their respective parents' warm embrace, with mouths opened slightly in muted wonder and surprise. It did not escape Becky's notice that Pierre's face was slightly flushed.

September

The Old Mill House glowed in the setting sun; its ancient mellow-yellow stone walls radiated warmth from the heat of the September day.

The following morning was the start of the new school year, and the children had been in bed and asleep by 6 o'clock; Polly and William needed no coaxing as they had spent the day rushing about like mad things in the garden and were exhausted.

Alone for the first time in many weeks, Becky sat musing on the swing-seat in the front garden, a glass of Sancerre turned the colour of ripe apricots by the setting sun's rays held in her right hand. Flake and Cadbury lay prostrate on the parched grass below Becky's outstretched feet also bathing in the warmth and glory of the sun.

Becky breathed in deeply and felt herself completely relax on the outward breath, at the same time whispering the word "Bliss…" Two tails softly thumped on the ground in response.

I have never known such perfect peace, or happiness for that matter, she mused, taking a small sip of the perfectly chilled wine.

The lightest and gentlest of breezes momentarily kissed Becky's upturned face in passing, then all was still again.

However, the air introduced a thought that knocked quietly on a door in the back of her mind and she felt anxiety flutter in her heart momentarily; a voice whispered, "…what about …No, not now, not just yet," willed Becky silently. "Tomorrow I will face 'all that' but now I will just be at peace, this much I deserve I know."

Slowly tucking her feet under her, Becky relaxed back onto the cushions of the old seat and sighing again deeply. "Heaven," she breathed.

* * *

The long journey from Nyons to Cherbourg had been largely uneventful except for regular stops for *'les boissons' 'quelque-chose a manger' et bien sur 'les toilettes!'* On the way down south, they had driven through the night but driving back through the heat of the day was a different kettle of fish altogether and the journey drained them all so that when they finally reached the ferry and had found their cabin, within minutes Becky, Polly and William were all sound asleep in their bunks.

It must have been a smooth crossing because Becky, waking briefly in the night from a pleasantly disturbing dream about Pierre, had the sensation of being propelled very gently across a great ocean that was both calm and smooth.

After a 'full English breakfast' at a little café just outside Wenstone, the intrepid travellers set off again, this time on the final, short leg of their journey home.

Liza and Bill greeted Becky, Polly and William with open arms as Flake and Cadbury danced and jumped around them, barking in excitement. Maurice appeared, yawning and stretching, from his favourite outdoor spot in the sun on top of the old stone wall surrounding the front garden. Looking up at Becky with adoring, if enquiring, eyes, Maurice wrapped himself around her legs purring like a tiger! Polly and William hugged their grandparents and then swooped off excitedly around the enclosed garden before tearing off in the direction of the large open garden at the back of the house!

"Coffee darling?" Liza beamed.

"Oui... I mean yes ... please, Mum! How wonderful to see you both, and looking so well!"

"And you too, Becky darling," said Bill. "I'm so glad—so much better than when you left."

"Yes Dad!" laughed Becky looking up at her father, as linking arms they followed Liza through the old wooden door at the side of the house to the sunny patio outside the conservatory at the back.

"Mum! Dad!" gasped Becky, "the garden looks fantastic!"

Lisa and Bill smiled at each other, looking pleased as they all sat down at the wooden table.

Coffee smelled divine, and Becky felt a sudden rush of emotion as the aroma transported her back to another garden and, it seemed, another life, until, blinking, she realised where she was and that it was not all a dream, and that Pierre was real, their budding relationship was real, and that life at last held real hope for her and the children.

She beamed happily at her mother and father who sat patiently watching her, and waiting.

"Well!" she sighed at last, looking with smiling eyes and lips at Lisa and Bill and then up at the blue sky above, "I think everything's going to be alright! In fact more than alright, it's going to be wonderful, you'll see!" Becky added looking from one to the other of her parents.

"You'll see," she repeated softly, "because we, that is, the children and I have become quite close to Pierre and his children—it's amazing isn't it, Mum? Dad?"

Lisa and Bill smiled gently at her; Lisa's well trained eye noticed her daughter's cheeks flushing slightly as she spoke Pierre's name. *Thank goodness*, she mused, *I see a ray of sunshine at last; I hope and pray something good and lasting comes from all this…poor darling, she has had a terrible time—she has a few more hurdles to go yet though…* as thoughts of Rob filtered into her mind and the memory of the curious visit two weeks ago…*I shall have to tell her*, thought Lisa…*but not now, not today…*

"We're going to spend Christmas in France!" announced Becky excitedly. "Imagine! And we're so excited! You don't mind do you, Mum? Dad?" She finished, a sudden anxious expression causing her forehead to furrow as she looked from one parent to the other; Becky was suddenly aware that in her exuberance she had forgotten about her parents and their long-established routine of them all spending Christmas together at the Old Mill House.

"No, no, darling, please, don't worry," said Lisa smiling gently. "What wonderful news, we shall be fine, you know we will! won't we, Bill?"

"Absolutely!" said Bill firmly, also smiling.

Relief flooded across Becky's troubled face. "Oh, that's wonderful," she breathed.

"And perhaps next year," she continued excitedly, "we can all have Christmas together, in France!"

"What a lovely idea!" laughed Lisa.

Bill hooted with laughter in his deep booming voice, whilst Becky giggled like a teenager!

Polly and William stopped mid-flight down the slope in the old apple orchard where they were wheeling about pretending to be aeroplanes, and stood for a few moments, wings askew, watching the adults below with eyes agog and mouths open.

"Everyone's happy when Daddy's not here," lisped Polly quietly.

William said nothing but sniffed loudly, he was impatient to complete his bombing raid.

"The garden is such a joy, Becky," smiled Lisa. "We so love being here, don't we, Bill?"

"Yes, yes, we do, very much," said Bill positively. "Must admit we've become very fond of the dogs, and Maurice too, of course! And it's been a real pleasure to look after hens again after so long. We might get three or four for us at home mightn't we, Ma?" He finished, winking at Becky's mother.

"Christmas shouldn't be a problem for us, should it darling?" Lisa asked looking her husband straight in the eye. "We can keep the heat on low at home in case it freezes, and it's so nice and warm and snug here with the fires and the aga! And Gina and Robin can always come here to be with us, you wouldn't mind darling, would you?"

"Mind? Absolutely not, Mum, of course, that's brilliant. Thank you both so so much!"

"Mmm, good idea," agreed Bill thoughtfully.

Lisa and Bill were due to return to their home 10 miles away in Claymoor St John the next day, their own garden was sorely in need of some care and attention, so Lisa decided she would tell Becky about the visit tonight, after supper, when the children were in bed.

But somehow Lisa never found the right moment to speak to Becky about Rob, nor had she the heart to break the spell of happiness. So, knowing she would definitely find the right time in the very near future to breach the subject of Rob's visit, she let the matter drop, for the time being.

"We'll let them settle down a bit, don't you think?" Lisa asked anxiously later when she and Bill were in bed reading.

"Good idea, old girl," Bill replied sleepily, his mind elsewhere, "don't need to mention it just yet…"

And soon he was snoring gently, book face down on his chest, specs still perched at the end of his nose.

Lisa gently removed Bill's specs, set his book upon the bedside table, and sighed deeply. Her eyes, wide open, gazed out of the open window at the night sky. The utter still and quiet of the night only served to emphasise the fact that her mind was not quiet and still but was whirling about like a tempest at sea. It was well after the old downstairs clock chimed 2 o'clock before Lisa eventually drifted into a fitful sleep.

"Mum!"

"Granny!"

Chorused Becky and the children as Lisa stepped gingerly out of the conservatory and into the garden. It was another perfect day, still and warm, with the promise of midday heat.

"My goodness gracious me, what time is it?" Lisa, blinking rapidly in the bright light.

"It's 11 o'clock, sleepyhead!" said Bill cheerfully, strolling across the lawn towards her holding a small wicker basket full to the brim with warm, dark brown eggs, and wearing a broad smile on his face.

"Granny! Granny! Come over here and see what we're doing! We've made a den in the shed for sick animals!" called out Polly excitedly.

"There's worms too, Gran-gran!" chimed in William who was jumping up and down in front of his grandmother.

"Wills, Polly, darlings, let poor Granny sit down at least! I'm sure she'll come and see the animal den later!"

"Hello Mum!" beamed Becky, giving her mother a big hug. "Coffee?"

"Oh, yes please," said Lisa, smiling gratefully at Becky.

"Right! Now just sit down and relax and I'll go and get that coffee—would you like a croissant too? I popped out to the baker earlier and we were lucky, he had just five left!" Becky continued breathlessly. Her mother merely nodded, smiled and sat down rather heavily on one of the cushioned loungers on the patio.

Coming to sit next to Lisa, very carefully holding onto the basket of eggs, Bill gently asked, "Alright, old thing?"

"Fine, yes thank you, darling," replied Lisa smiling thinly. "Just a little tired this morning but I'll be fine in a jiffy. Coffee and a croissant, how delicious! Now, let me see, what have you got there. My goodness that must be a record number of eggs! And aren't they so beautifully brown? As brown as Becky and the children!" she continued, laughing at the thought. Lisa was beginning to feel a little better.

"Coffee will be most welcome, and then my darling we must see to packing up and think of leaving at about 2.30. We'll need to pick up milk and bread and something for supper in the village on the way home. I must say though…"

Lisa was thinking as she spoke that she would love to stay another night as she was feeling really very tired indeed, when Becky interrupted her thoughts and words, as, placing coffee, mugs and a large jug of hot milk on the table, she cried, "Oh do please stay another night, Mummy, Daddy—it's such a beautiful day, and we can spend it all together; it's not often we get the opportunity with the children at school and me working. So, how about it? One special day all together, just relaxing—I'll nip off to the supermarket after we've had coffee, and I can pick up anything you need for home for tomorrow, so you won't have to stop anywhere, just go straight home and settle back in! Please say yes!" Becky finished excitedly, she was almost jumping up and down in her enthusiasm.

"Oh alright darling!" said Lisa laughing, "that's fine with us isn't it, Bill?"

"Absolutely!" beamed Becky's father.

And so, they all did have the happiest of days together, doing not a lot, just relaxing and talking and drinking and eating and laughing! Becky went food shopping before lunch, leaving her parents relaxing in the garden watching with much amusement the antics of the children and their erstwhile patients.

After an English-ingredient version of a Salade Niçoise with chunks of fried bread and crispy bacon to decorate the dish, and a glass or two of elderflower champagne that she had made earlier in the summer, Becky, her father and her mother relaxed on the sun-loungers with more coffee and the newspapers whilst the children lay on rugs reading, with the dogs flopped down beside them. Soon, Bill drifted off into sleep, and Becky and her mother talked quietly together, remembering the people and places of Becky's childhood in Sussex, their frequent giggles floating gently on the warm, fragrant air.

The following day dawned hot and still again. Today however, Lisa was up and about with the rest of the family at 7 o'clock. She had slept deeply and dreamlessly, having decided the afternoon before to ring Becky about their visitor, on the children's first day back at school. Lisa was dreading the whole thing, but at least Becky is so much stronger now, she told herself, but she must be told before she finds out any other way. Lisa began to panic again as she conjured up visions of Becky ringing the police to inform them of a burglary when she found the train set had vanished. *No*, she said firmly to herself, *I'll be ringing her in only 24 hours. She won't have noticed the missing train set hopefully, the drawing room's more or less shut up at this time of year, and fingers crossed William's too engrossed elsewhere to bother.*

I know exactly what to do, I'll ring her tomorrow morning as soon as she gets back to the house from dropping the children off. Hopefully, I'll catch her having a cup of coffee. It has to be then because she starts work again on Wednesday morning...

Her plan of action settled and its place marked firmly in her mental diary, Lisa and Bill spent a further relaxing morning at the Old Mill House, before setting off for home after an early lunch.

With Polly and William still engrossed in their by now very messy animal hospital den, Becky set about making preparations for the following morning, putting out school uniforms and sorting mounds of washing; ahead lay the new school year and there were new plans to be made! She was grateful to Leo for telephoning at tea-time to say 'welcome home to La Grande Bretagne' but this was swiftly followed by a curt '…look forward to a report of your findings… Wednesday morning, 9.30 sharp!' before the line went dead with a loud click leaving Becky a little put-out.

"Good morning, darling! Sleep well? Children get off to school OK?…Oh, that's wonderful, it just shows what a bit of rest and relaxation away from it all can do!"

"Yes, Mummy! It's so true!" replied Becky cheerfully.

She hasn't called me Mummy for years thought Lisa, not since before she was married in fact. Oh Lord I wish I didn't have to pour cold water on this fire…

"How are you and Daddy? Nice to be back home I expect, although I know you feel very much at home here now," chatted Becky happily, thinking how lovely it had been to have her parents to stay and feeling glad that they had obviously enjoyed their time.

They've never been so relaxed here and to think they're absolutely fine about staying here over Christmas whilst we're in France…

The thought of France—and Pierre—infused Becky with bubbles of pure joy.

I can't believe this is all happening! and I never realised such happiness existed until now'

"Darling? Becky? Are you still there?"

"Oh, Mummy! I am sorry, I just got carried away on a cloud of happy thoughts! And I really am so grateful, more than I can say, that you and Daddy are coming to stay for Christmas; I'm just over the moon you're both so relaxed and happy being here now. It's unbelievable, everything's turning out magically!"

Lisa laughed and before she could reply, Becky continued in a more serious tone,

"You know what, Mum? I'm really very glad now that Rob left and went to London, things had been pretty bad between us for much more than just this last year, since Wills was about two actually, everything sort of started to fall apart at the seams around then…"

Lisa caught her breath; this was the first time Becky had made any comment at all to her about Rob and his abrupt departure. A vision of a deep, dark ravine appeared in front of Lisa's eyes … *Not now, I'm not going to ask any questions about all that yet …*

For years, Lisa had intuitively felt, as only a mother can, undercurrents of strain, tension and fear running through the threads of Becky and Rob's relationship, and for a long time she had worried about Becky and of course about the children, and whilst she never talked to Bill about it she guessed that he too was aware of there being something 'not quite right'.

"Talking of Rob," said Lisa calmly, "I've been meaning to tell you since you got back from France but somehow never quite found the right time, but I have to tell you, darling, that he called at the house about two weeks ago, to pick up a few things he said…"

"What?" Becky exploded. "You mean he came here? To the house? Whilst you were here? And we were away?"

"Yes, yes, Becky darling, now please, just let me tell you what happened."

"Oh my God!" exhaled Becky violently.

"Becky!"

"Yes, sorry, Mum, carry on, tell me the worst."

"Well, Dad and I were just sitting down to have a cup of coffee in the garden, it was a lovely hot day I remember, when we heard Rob's voice calling out, rather rudely I thought 'Who's here?' Well, we both jumped out of our skins but got up and went to greet him. He was standing in the kitchen doorway, and he seemed in a hurry. I think I said to him, or was it Dad? I can't remember now…"

"It doesn't matter, Mum, just tell me what happened," interrupted Becky abruptly.

"OK," continued Lisa patiently, "So anyway we said it was nice to see him and asked him how he was. But as I said he seemed in a fearful hurry, and after pompously telling us that his sister has converted her basement into a luxury apartment for him with his own private entrance and, oh yes, that he was now working full-time at some advertising agency or other, he said he'd just come to pick up a few of his things. I did catch sight of a small white van parked outside. Anyway, he asked us no questions at all, about you or the children or anything, and disappeared abruptly into the house saying something about his trainset."

Becky gasped at this, but Lisa continued quickly before she could interrupt further,

"... Dad and I went back into the garden. I caught a glimpse of him carrying an armful of clothes. He must have been at the house for about half an hour I suppose, and just shouted out to us from the conservatory that he was off and to tell you he had taken the photo albums."

"What? How could he? How dare he? Mum, why didn't you stop him?" Becky wailed.

"I'm so sorry, darling, there was very little we could do, he was gone in a flash, in fact, by the time we reached the conservatory, we could hear the van speeding away. I did check, darling, and I'm afraid the train set has gone."

"Oh God," groaned Becky, "Mum, what do I do? Wills loves the train set, even though Rob never let him play with it on his own, but how mean, how could he do it? And the photo albums, how dare he?"

"Perhaps, he'll set up the train set in his new place for Wills to play with when he visits his father," said Lisa mildly, attempting to bring Becky's focus on to the reality of her situation, for she intuitively knew that Rob was gone for good.

"Oh my God!" exclaimed Becky, "I hadn't thought of that. Oh, Mum, what am I going to do?"

"Just put one foot in front of the other, like you always do, and everything will sort itself out for the best, you'll see," replied Lisa with a confidence she did not feel at all, as visions of the deep, dark ravine threatened her sunshine once again. "One step at a time, my darling, think positive, stay calm, and remember you are not alone!"

"Thank you, Mum," replied Becky, more like her old self, having regained her composure from listening to her mother's calm and soothing voice, "for everything, you and Dad, for always being there for us, where would we be without you?"

"We're always just at the end of the phone, and we'll be seeing you again very soon, William's birthday coming up? Just focus on the future and those two precious children of yours and all will be well. Must dash, darling, love you lots, and Becky, please ring me whenever you need to talk."

"Bye, Mum, and thanks again."

"Bye, darling, and good luck at work tomorrow!"

Becky stood for a moment, a fixed stare glued to the receiver, before replacing it quietly and firmly into its place. Turning slowly, she walked straight out of the house, and into the garden and the bright sunlight; secateurs in hand, Becky spent the next two hours amongst her beloved flowers, pruning and cutting until she had armfuls of dahlias, roses, mombresia and gypsophilia which she intended to arrange in flower vases later. Becky planned to fill the whole house with flowers, placing the vases in each and every room, as witness to her determination to ensure a secure and happy future for herself and the children. There were now mounds of old stems and stalks beside each flower bed which would have to be moved to the compost heap or the bonfire place later; at the moment however an unusually spritely Maurice was playing cat and mouse with one particular pile, stalking then pouncing before rushing away and up the nearest tree. Flake and Cadbury however seemed more sensitive to Becky's mood and followed her about like faithful soldiers standing guard.

At ten past three, Becky locked up the house and bolted the doors before setting off at a leisurely pace to collect the children from school.

* * *

"Mummy! Mummy!" shrieked Polly and William as they spotted Becky arriving at the school gates.

"Hey, slow down, tigers!" laughed Becky as the children catapulted into her open arms.

"Now, one at a time, how was it?" she beamed, first turning her attention to Polly then to William who was jumping up and down like a jack-in-a-box.

"Me first! Me first!" shouted William.

"No, darling," said Becky firmly, "I think Polly first, don't you?"

She had noticed a brief cloud waft across Polly's shining face. Becky knew that her astute and sometimes serious little girl often retreated when in any sort of subliminal competition. She knew Polly's thoughts ran deep and that she was bottling up many emotions concerning her father. Becky nonetheless recognised that William too, whilst always energetic, open and on the go, was also probably very puzzled as to his father's whereabouts and behaviour. Sighing deeply, Becky also recognised that things were much better 'out than in' and that their current situation was vastly better than when Rob had been at home and silent. Smiling broadly and kindly at William and placing a protective arm around his small shoulders, Becky turned all her attention towards Polly as placing her right arm around

Polly's shoulders, she focussed all her love and attention on her sensitive little daughter.

Polly relaxed, and smiling up at Becky took her thumb out of her mouth and said brightly :

"Miss Gentle is very nice, Mummy, she's kind and sort of funny. We did some sewing and some drawing and some writing! And Mummy!" said Polly jumping up and down, "We're going to do cooking!—weeeeeeeeeeeee…" and with that Polly aeroplaned off around the playground, eventually finding a little friend and giving her a hug before flying back to Becky and William.

"That's Jemima, Mum!" said Polly breathlessly, "she's new and she's my best friend!"

Knowing how fleeting these 'best friend' relationships often were, Becky smiled delightedly and replied, "Polls, how lovely, and Jemima is such a nice name!" thinking privately that a name like Jemima could be a disaster for the little girl with all its duck associations. So, hugging Polly tightly and taking hold of her hand, Becky turned all her attention to a William whom she now noticed had turned uncharacteristically quiet. He stood gazing up at the sky, squinting, although it had clouded over whilst Becky was walking to school.

"Wills!" exclaimed Becky brightly, "And how was your day, darling?" William blinked and slowly turned towards Becky as if coming out of a trance, before opening his eyes very wide as looking up at her smiling face said in an excited tone, "Mum! Can I get some glasses?"

Becky failed completely to check a look of combined surprise, anxiety and fear that briefly flashed across her face, before gathering her composure and replying brightly,

"Why, William darling, what makes you think you need glasses?"

A snort from William brought sniggers from Polly.

"Cos my friend Charlie, he wears specs and he can see much better than me!" shouted William.

"Right, OK, I see," replied Becky slowly. "We'll have to get your eyes tested and get you some specs like Charlie's perhaps. Poor sausage, I never realised, silly Mummy," continued Becky quite seriously, although she had doubts as to whether William needed specs at all, but she decided to go along with this.

Goodness knows what goes on in their little minds, she thought, inwardly sighing, outwardly smiling.

"Yippee!" shouted William. "C'mon, Mum, sweets after school!"

"You said!" chorused Polly and William.

"Alright, alright!" laughed Becky. "Off we go then!"

It wasn't until they were halfway home and all was quiet as the children munched and sucked happily, that Becky remembered that she had meant to have a word with Miss Clasby, still William's form teacher.

Poor lady, mused Becky, *I hope she had a good, long rest over the holidays. I'll catch up with her soon and ask what she thinks about William's eyesight…although I'd better get his sight checked, just in case…*

Just as Becky's mind started drifting across the Channel towards Pierre and as she felt excitement mounting at the thought of hearing his enticing, foreign voice over the phone later, William hiccoughed loudly before spitting into the hedge a half-chewed green jelly baby and exclaiming loudly,

"Mum! Mr Frog was frothing and spitting today, d'you think he swallowed some soap for his breakfast?" William chortled as he remembered the livid red face and pivoting eyeballs of headmaster Mr Faulkner at first-day-of-term assembly.

"No, don't be thilly, Wills," lisped Polly. "He wasth telling us all to be good and behave but histh face thuddenly went red and he thstarted thpitting when you put up your hand and asthked to go to the *pissoir*, you know, Mum, like boys do in France when they want to pee-pee."

Becky inwardly groaned; this was not a good way for William to set foot into the new school year. *If only the headmaster were not such an apparently volatile person, when it came to explain to Mr Faulkner that we are having a few family problems at the moment, or for that matter perhaps I should have a word with him myself...*

"Wills, darling, I think," said Becky continuing to walk but taking hold of William's hand, "I think it would be best if from now on you tried very hard to be very good at school and also tried very hard not to upset Headmaster—you see he's a very busy man and you need to be like a mouse when he's in the room…"

"Squeak, squeak!" laughed William before stuffing two orange jelly babies into his mouth and humming loudly.

"Oh, dear," said Becky, to no-one in particular.

Polly just smiled up at her mother before skipping the rest of the way home!

* * *

"Becky!" called out Fizz, straightening her back and raising a rubber-gloved hand from the middle of the slightly faded but still colourful herbaceous border.

Becky changed tack and walked across the newly mown lawn towards her.

"Hello, Fizz!" said Becky enthusiastically, deciding that perhaps it was quite nice after all to be back, although 99% of her wished to be in France. That one percent would have to suffice, it would be enough she assured herself.

"How lovely to see you, Becky!" said Fizz. "And you look amazing, so brown! I'd be almost envious if it weren't for the fact that we're off to Pierre's next week for ten days! Can't wait!"

Becky stopped short, ten feet from where Fizz stood beaming, gardening trowel in hand.

"Oh! I didn't know," she exclaimed, fortunately managing to stifle a jealous tone that rose unbidden like bile, threatening to burn the back of her throat with sulphurous fumes; the sensation was of a volcano on the verge of erupting.

"Yes, yes," said Fizz, bending down again to the task in hand. "We decided last night actually," she continued, briefly glancing up at Becky who thought at that moment that Fizz looked just like a tortoise poking its head out of its shell. "Leo's booked the flight to Nice, and Pierre's going to meet us!".

"D'you know what, Becky?" Fizz continued, straightening her back once more and squinting in thought up at the mottled grey sky, "I wouldn't mind staying on for a bit, having a real break; I'm sure Pierre wouldn't mind, I know him so well…" she added dreamily.

Becky's jaw had slowly but surely been dropping as Fizz continued her prattling and her mouth was now wide open.

"What on earth's the matter, Becky?" Fizz said suddenly and sharply. She had come out of her reverie without warning and was now glaring at Becky, who in turn blushed bright red before stammering awkwardly, "Must be off, I'll be late, Leo'll think I'm not coming…"

Heart pounding, with what Becky shamefully could only recognise as a surprising attack of jealousy brought on by Fizz's news, she quickly turned and raced across the lawn towards the house.

Fizz merely shrugged and smiling to herself returned her attention to the garden, humming softly the opening bars of 'Un Homme et Une Femme.'

"Becky! There you are!" bellowed Leo from the top of the staircase outside the office. "Where the bloody helluv you been? It's 10 o'clock already, for Chrissake."

"Oh hi, Leo," responded Becky breathlessly as she ran up the stairs two at a time, "nice to see you too," she added sarcastically, "talking to Fizz as a matter of fact," she continued, angrily pushing past an open-mouthed Leo into the bright little office.

"Well, charmed, I'm sure," muttered Leo, yanking back his chair and sitting down rather heavily.

Silence reigned for two minutes.

"I'll start on that report then," said Becky coldly, as she switched on her computer, taking a large, chunky notebook out of her bulging bag.

"Oh, for God's sake, woman," said Leo wearily.

"For God's sake yourself," was the gritty response.

Sighing heavily and noisily, Leo said, "Look, sorry about the barking. How did it all go by the way?" he continued, quite gently for Leo. "Hear you two hit it off, got on like a proverbial house on fire!" he finished loudly, a smile on his face, elbows on the desk and his two forefingers tapping together rhythmically.

Oh hell, thought Becky, *he's trying to draw me out. Must keep up the barriers.*

"I don't know what you mean, Leo," said Becky frostily. "Pierre is very hospitable and as you know we covered a great deal of ground, on your behalf," she finished emphatically.

"Yes," said Leo slowly. "Quite," he finished, sighing again heavily, before replacing his glasses on the tip of his long nose.

"Email a copy each of that report to me and to Pierre if you would please, just as soon as you've finished and checked it over of course."

"Of course," repeated Becky curtly, turning her attention 100% to the task in hand.

"Fizz tell you, did she?" Leo asked casually five minutes later, watching Becky over the top of *Wine Connoisseurs Monthly*, like the fox watching Jemima Puddleduck over the top of his newspaper as she waddled towards him unsuspecting and innocent.

"Sorry?" Becky replied distantly, not looking up from her computer screen.

"I said," retorted Leo, clearly needled by Becky's obtuse behaviour.

"I said," he repeated, more loudly this time, "did Fizz tell you then? About our trip to France next week?"

"What? Oh that, yes, she did as a matter of fact," replied Becky, glaring at Leo for a split second. "Why?" She questioned rather rudely.

Ha, got her, Leo chuckled inwardly.

"No, no, nothing really," sighed Leo undramatically, stifling a yawn and returning his attention to the wine magazine.

"Pierre's always fancied my wife," he continued after a few moments, not looking up from his page, "told me so himself, you know. Must have an Oedipus complex or some such thing, Fizz's nearly old enough to be his mother. Perverted if you ask me," he concluded dryly, swiftly and for only a second fixing Becky with a glare.

Despite trying to keep her defences up, Becky thought she caught a minute flash of sadness in that swift look.

What the hell's going on here? Becky panicked uncertainly.

"I'm not sure I understand what you mean, Leo," she replied warily, trying desperately to hold on to a calm and confident persona in the midst of this rapidly unfolding drama. She clung on with all her mental and emotional might to the reality that she knew. She could in no way go down the path to doubt and confusion. *No,* she told herself, *I know what I know, and what I feel, and I have to trust this. This is just about two eccentric, probably bored, middle-aged people with a flair for dramatics. That's all it is,* she relaxed, taking a deep breath.

Maybe Fizz is a little infatuated with Pierre, but then who wouldn't be, and why not?

"Right!" said Leo abruptly, standing up and sending his chair crashing into the wall behind him. "I'm off to that vintners meeting, Becky. You're in charge. Get that report finished today would you if you can? Not sure when I'll be back. "

And with that, Leo banged out of the office and thundered down the stairs. Becky had to restrain herself from rushing to the office door and gawking at her retreating boss; ever since tumbling down the stairs on that fateful night when she first met Pierre, Becky had felt a frisson of tingling fear every time she, or anyone else for that matter, descended to the ground floor.

Inhaling deeply and exhaling loudly, and with puffed out cheeks, Becky returned to the computer and the report writing, a stubborn and determined expression on her face.

October

Gentle, warm September moved swiftly into October and with it the first chill winds of the coming winter.

It wasn't until the second week of the month that Becky finally managed to track down Miss Clasby, who was surprised that Becky appeared not to have registered William squinting as he read.

"I wonder, Mrs Saunders," asked the kind lady, "have you noticed William holding his books close to his face when he's reading, or bending over to write with his face only a few inches from the page?"

"Er, well, quite honestly no I hadn't," replied a slightly flustered Becky, taken completely by surprise. She had been expecting and dreading to learn about another ink episode.

"I, we…" she stammered weakly, "we haven't done too much reading together at home lately. I'm afraid it's all been a bit hectic, with one thing and another … But actually, now I come to think of it, he did ask if he could have glasses like his friend Charlie the other day…" Becky carried on lamely.

By now Becky's face was turning the colour of ripe strawberries as she experienced waves of guilt over her conspicuous failure as a parent. *Single parent at that*, she mentally retorted to herself, before gathering her fast failing wits about her and replying firmly, looking Miss Clasby directly in the eye;

"Well then, Miss Clasby, thank you very much. I have been meaning to make an eye appointment for him for a few weeks but shall now arrange it as soon as possible. Thank you, I do appreciate you bringing this to my attention!" she finished, smiling grimly.

On returning home and once the children were munching toast and marmite in front of the television, Becky gave her mother a quick ring.

"Mum! How are you both? Oh good. Yes, we're really looking forward to Saturday too!…Before you go, I was just wondering do you have the phone number by you of your optician?…Oh good, yes I've got that…No, it's nothing serious but I just need to get William's eyes tested, he's apparently been squinting at school. Listen, must dash, I'll ring them now and see if I can get something for Saturday. See you then, lots of love!"

* * *

Despite a night of tossing and turning, Becky was up and about early and had collected the eggs and fed all the animals before waking Polly and William. She felt the beginnings of a dull headache as they sat munching cereal quietly in the kitchen, but she was grateful when it gradually receded with each cup of tea. Becky had four cups, each with two teaspoons of sugar, something she never usually did.

"Right, my darlings!" she said briskly, sweeping plates and cutlery off the kitchen table and into the sink with a loud clatter. "Time to clean teeth and then off we go!"

"Whoopee!" was the response as William followed by Polly tore upstairs and along the landing to the back bathroom.

It seemed like no more than two minutes later when Becky's two little birds swooped downstairs again, faces shining with excitement at the prospect of the coming day. Treats were definitely in store and the cold drizzly weather did nothing to dampen their spirits as they all piled into the car.

William was to have his eyes tested in the little town of Orcheston half way between home and Bill and Lisa's house. The optician, a kindly, balding, middle-aged man had read the signs accurately.

"Mm," he pondered seriously, after completing the test. "Now, whilst I am pleased to say I can find no serious sight problem," turning from Becky to William, he concluded, "I think we need to set you up with a pair of reading glasses young man."

Mouth open, William merely nodded his head up and down at least five times. Becky suspected that this was because William was overawed with the eye-testing equipment, the test he had just undergone, and the shining round hairless head and face of the optician. This was a banquet indeed for William's overactive imagination.

Mr Pickles pulled out a drawer at the very top of a gleaming glass cabinet full of spectacles.

"Now, just try these for size, William," motioned the kindly gentleman, placing the shiny new spectacles in their thin tortoiseshell frame, onto William's nose.

"Yes, I think these are just the right size. Now, can you see the letters on this sheet clearly, William?" Mr Pickles concluded.

William nodded slowly, before smiling broadly at Mr Pickles.

"Good! That's that then!" said the optician, smiling at William. "Let me know how he gets on, Mrs Saunders," continued Mr Pickles turning to Becky, the shadow of a wink causing his left eyelid to flicker slightly.

Becky smiled and thanked Mr Pickles before the three of them stepped out into the street once more.

"Now, Polls, that pair of fluffy pink rabbit slippers I promised you, some flowers for granny, chocolate for grandpa, then off we go to lunch!"

"Yes, yes, yes!" cried Polly jumping up and down excitedly.

William meanwhile was unusually quiet, looking around slowly, practising being 'a person who wears glasses.'

"Will gran and gramps notice d'you think, Mum?" He asked, looking up at Becky, a serious expression on his face.

"What, darling?" Becky asked, miles away in France. "…oh, of course, Wills, I'm sure they will notice you have glasses, they've been very concerned about you."

A little pleased 'Mmm' escaped Williams's nose, before he fell into complete silence throughout the remainder of the shopping trip and also the rest of the way to his grandparents' house.

"Granny! Grandpa!" shouted out Polly, jumping, hopping and skipping up the little paved garden path.

Becky, walking quickly behind her, clutching a large multi-coloured bunch of mixed flowers, turned to grab William's hand as it trailed through the bushes and shrubs at the side of the path.

"Here we are at last!" laughed Becky as she hugged first her mother who was wiping her hands quickly on her flowered apron, then her smiling father who padded over in his thick gumboot socks to greet them.

"And here you all are!" cried Lisa bending down to hug an ecstatic Polly and admire her beautiful slippers that she had put on the minute she stepped indoors.

"Ah, William, there you are, my boy!" said Bill loudly, with a broad smile on his face. "Come on over here and show me those spectacles of yours. My, my, what a big boy you look, and very clever with it if I might say!" he finished seriously.

"I'm very glad to see you have your glasses now, William. I know I'd be lost without mine!" said his grandmother kindly, extending her arms to give William a hug, before turning to a bouncing Polly to give her another equally big hug.

"Now, I'm just about to dish up, so if you'd all like to wash your hands," Lisa continued looking hard at Bill who nearly always forgot, "and sit at the table, I'll bring in the lunch!"

Delicious smells wafted through from the kitchen and it wasn't long before a feast lay upon the dining room table—golden, crispy-skinned roast chicken, roast and boiled potatoes, buttered carrots sprinkled with parsley, asparagus, peas and broad beans (frozen but all from the garden), bread sauce and a steaming jug of delicious-smelling gravy.

There was homemade apple pie and cream for desert, with chilled white wine for the grown-ups and sweet apple juice for the children.

Polly and William were so intent on the delicious food that they barely said a word.

"You can get down now, children," said Lisa kindly when she noticed empty pudding plates. "You know where the toys are darlings, don't you?"

"Yes! Granny!" they chorused, and immediately rushed off in the direction of the spacious conservatory where stood a large toy box.

The adults were just about to carry on talking when William's head appeared round the dining room door; "Thank you for lunch!" he said clearly, in a serious tone looking at the three of them over the top of his new glasses.

"That's very kind of you, William, I'm glad you enjoyed it," replied his grandmother in equally serious tone.

And with that, the door shut.

Becky stifled hysterical giggles that rose up unbidden; but it really was not a laughing matter, hysterical maybe but definitely not funny, in the least.

"The optician was so kind. He just knew exactly what to do and what to say. I'm so grateful to him. I suppose he comes across this sort of thing every now and again," said Becky wistfully, staring out of the window.

Lisa imperceptibly nodded at Bill who said kindly, "I'm sure he does darling, and I'm sure it's not that unusual, and it's quite a good thing really because it allows William a genuine excuse for attention and sympathy too, which I know he gets from us all. But also in an odd way, the glasses give him some protection; they're something he can hide behind if and when he feels vulnerable which—and you don't need me to tell you Becks, he must from time to time feel without his father at his side."

"I wonder if both children think Rob's disappearing like that, after being so quiet and cut off for so long, is because of something they've done? I wonder if they feel they've done something wrong and that's why he's gone," queried Becky in a quivery voice, "I've read somewhere that children can feel guilty and blame themselves …" trailing off into silence.

"Oh no darling, I'm sure that can't be right!" exclaimed Lisa.

Becky raised her head, looking slowly from one parent to the other.

"Well," she sighed heavily, "it's better to face that possibility. You never know what goes on in their little heads. I must just do all I can to protect them and make life as happy as I possibly can. The tough bit's to come I suppose, but I'll just have to weather it. I'm so very glad you're both here, I don't know what I'd do without you" she tailed off, struggling against a tidal wave of grief that threatened to engulf her. From nowhere, her visionary dream that seemingly long ago January night, swam into her consciousness, giving Becky the strength to regain her composure now as she had eventually regained her confidence then, following that stormy night.

"I'm sure it's just a phase," she continued brightly, noticing imperceptible relaxing of foreheads and jawbones as she spoke; Becky smiled at first her mother and then her father. "Must think positive, as you always taught me! And there's so much to look forward to!"

The spell was broken as Becky, Lisa and Bill relaxed at last, and started chatting about the weather, and also about the fact that Christmas was fast approaching! At which thought, Lisa jumped up and announced, "Coffee!" before trundling the laden trolley through and into the kitchen, firmly closing the door behind her.

When Lisa was out of the room, Bill suddenly said to Becky, "You know I remember the time we had to sell up everything, your Ma and I, not long after you and Jonathan were born …we eventually made it through though," he continued softly and thoughtfully. "We're here now but it was tough at the time I can tell you … seems life's all about learning the hard way!" he finished with a wry smile, and a loving pat on Becky's outstretched hand.

"… wish you'd had someone half decent and unselfish by your side these last few years, Becks."

"I know, Dad, so do I. I wonder what made me marry him in the first place actually, he always did have a filthy temper, under that calm, charming exterior. I didn't know then what I know now though," she said quietly.

The dining room fell silent, except for the steady ticking of the beautiful old clock on the mantelpiece; Becky quietly contemplating what she had just said out loud for the first time, whilst Bill struggled with coming to terms with his daughter's revealing confession, trying to sort out in his head what was the best thing to say at this moment. He was just about to continue the conversation by saying again that, 'it really does seem, we all have to learn the hard way,' when he changed his mind, rose up out of his chair and, bending over to kiss the top of his daughter's head, said gently,

"We're always here for you, you know, you and those two lovely little children of yours."

Becky turned her head and looked lovingly up at her father, "Thank you Dad. I know now why you said 'goodbye' to me when you gave me away at the wedding"

A look of deep love and understanding infused the kind old man's handsome face.

"Coffee!" trilled Lisa's voice from the depths of the kitchen.

"Ah! Orders!" joked Bill, making his way towards the door from the dining room into the kitchen, leaving Becky with a smile on her face.

Before making her way obediently to the comforts of the sitting room and the newspapers, Becky headed off to the conservatory to check on Polly and William who were ominously quiet. She was confronted however by a peaceful scene; the children had made a den with the big old toy box at the back and a small chair each side, one big old rug draped over the top and another cosy rug and several cushions on the floor inside the 'den.' Both were completely engrossed in and surrounded by dozens of books.

Breathing a sigh of relief, Becky retreated to relax in one of the big armchairs by the fire in the sitting room, with her feet up and a newspaper spread out in front of her.

"Here you are, darling," murmured Lisa ten minutes later, placing a steaming and aromatic cup of coffee on the table beside her.

"Mmm, thank you Mum," replied Becky sleepily, as she watched her father bend down and put a lighted match to the well-laid fire in the grate.

The flames leapt up the chimney as first the sticks and then the coal quickly caught light. Before long, the delicious warmth and comforting sounds of the fire enveloped them all as Becky, followed by Bill and then finally Lisa drifted into sleep.

November

The clocks went back and with the time change, from summertime to wintertime, came the fog followed swiftly on its heels by the frost. Becky now drove the children to school, picking them up on her way home from work. Flake and Cadbury patiently endured their erratic walk routine and often had to make do with twice daily skirmishes amongst the bushes and on the grassy slopes of the Old Mill House garden.

Becky was frequently visited by acute pangs of guilt that her beloved dogs were not getting all the attention and care they needed and deserved.

Purely temporary, purely temporary, she repeated to herself like a mantra. *I'll soon make it up to them. We just need to take each day as it comes and stay positive!*

Pierre, Patrick-Antoine and Francelle were conversely enjoying beautiful warm, sunny days, although the nights were cold now apparently.

Leo and Fizz returned tanned and reasonably relaxed from their visit. Fizz positively oozed confidence from every pore, much more so than usual, her infatuation with Pierre no secret, and whilst Leo shrugged it all off with a raised bushy eyebrow or two, Becky noticed he was downing more than one glass of wine at lunchtime, something he had never done before, or to her knowledge at least. Fizz refused the wine, drinking only chilled Perrier water with ice and a razor-thin slice of lemon.

"...such an exquisitely sensual drink, don't you think?" She said huskily to no one in particular, "...alcohol at lunchtime is so bad for the complexion and robs the vitality, mmm hot afternoons with no vitality, what a waste!"

"That's enough, Fizz," said Leo sharply. "I'm sure Becky's no interest in your meanderings."

"What on earth do you mean?" Fizz said lazily, a slanted smile on her face.

Becky felt, on these now quite frequent occasions, that she must look like a startled hen as she muttered her excuses and whisked herself away upstairs to the comparative calm of the office, blocking out all unpleasant thoughts and images that threatened to swim into her consciousness whenever she encountered Fizz and Leo together since their return.

It never used to be like this, she sighed before firmly shutting that particular door.

Since their return, however, Becky noticed that Leo was not as bombastic nor as enthusiastic as he 'normally' was, but then she reasoned, *he's been away relaxing, it happens to us all when we unwind...*

Although Becky spoke to Pierre only every other weekend, they always picked up where they left off. She had no reason to believe that things were anything but how they had been when they were together throughout the long hot summer. It was this strength of feeling and the sense of hope that went hand in hand with it that gave Becky the courage and the will to carry on as she did. She refused to entertain anything other than the perfect future she had imprinted in her memory. Even Leo's occasional sarcastic remarks about Pierre's drinking habits and womanising ways failed to dent her faith in him or dim the bright future she held in her heart of their lives joining together and of them all sailing happily ever after into the glowing sunset.

And the more she entertained these thoughts, the more she consciously knew that her marriage to Rob was at an end.

Becky began to trust that her feelings were the buds of real love, and she even dared also to trust that Pierre felt the same way about her.

Becky's faith in Pierre and her own feelings for him, and her belief that soon, after a few technicalities were overcome, she and the children would be moving to France, never for one moment dimmed. And this complete faith got her through each day, and the happiness it gave her radiated out and embraced her two children. She felt invincible, and protected, and for the first time in her life truly loved by a man whom she loved with all her heart. Becky knew that whatever lay ahead, that love would see them through and keep them safe. This love was her shield, and protected by it she blossomed, her confidence growing daily.

Becky was glad November had arrived for all its murkiness, because she could now say to herself, *next month we'll be together, next month we go to France!*

* * *

It was fortunate for Becky that she had a coat of armour, for on the morning of Bonfire Night her life was to erupt like a massive exploding firework threatening the wellbeing and safety of her little family.

The bombshell arrived with a dull thud on the hall floor together with an icy blast of cold air from outside. Even the dogs barked jumpily in surprise, racing to the front door to repel any threatening intruder and sniffing suspiciously the large white official-looking envelope.

"Mummy! Mummy!" shrieked Polly and William in unison.

"There's a huge thing from Bonfire Man!" shouted William in Becky's left ear as she knelt by the fireplace collecting last night's cinders.

Becky let out an involuntary shriek and leapt to her feet.

"Weeeeeee, wizzy cafrin wheels!" sang Polly, jumping up and down in front of her bewildered mother.

Becky laughed nervously as she hugged the children, at the same time removing the envelope from William's chocolate-spread fingers.

"Darlings! Look at the time!" she suddenly gasped. "Upstairs quickly! Wash hands, clean teeth, coats and hats on, we must go, we're late!"

I'll deal with that later, whatever it is, Becky thought as she placed the sticky envelope on the mantelpiece in the sitting room. *Thank goodness I've got today off.*

"Car children! Now!" Becky called up the stairs.

"Coming!" was the loud reply in unison.

Flake and Cadbury started barking loudly, picking up the urgency in Becky's voice.

"That's enough, girls!" she shouted. "Baskets! I'll take you out when I get back," she finished in a gentler tone.

The five-minute car journey to school in fact took much longer than usual. The roads were icy and a thick mist was now steadily rolling in off the marshes.

Fortunately, most children were late arriving due to the weather which was a huge relief to Becky and Polly, although William appeared totally unbothered, engaged as he was gazing out of the car window raising and lowering his glasses for the various alternative views this activity offered, and humming tunelessly to himself.

* * *

"Phew!" exclaimed Becky as she let herself into the house again by the ancient back door.

Walking into the kitchen, she was greeted ecstatically by Flake and Cadbury who were positively smiling in anticipation of a good long walk.

"Now, girls, you can go out in the garden for now whilst I have a quick cup of coffee and read this letter! Hmm," she continued to herself, not noticing the disappointed look on both dogs' faces. Becky opened the conservatory door to let them out into the garden, all the while staring thoughtfully at the white envelope she had retrieved from the mantelpiece. "I wonder who on earth this is from."

Sitting comfortably in her chair by the warm Aga, Becky poured herself a cup of strong, hot, black coffee, and taking a large gulp she started to open her post.

Soon be drinking French coffee! she thought excitedly, so *much better than…*

"Oh my God!" Becky shrieked, dropping her cup on the floor where it smashed to pieces, splashing coffee into every corner of the kitchen.

She gaped at the smart letterhead, 'Fitchington, Smith, Wilbur & Partners, Solicitors' was embossed in funereal black lettering onto the thick white paper '…Gray's Inn Road, London WC1…'

Dear Madam,

We are instructed by our client Mr Robert Saunders to issue divorce proceedings against you and to advise you that our client has also instructed us to pursue for sole custody of your two children on the grounds of your unreasonable and irresponsible behaviour, including adultery.

We are also advised by our client to inform you that he is claiming 75% of your joint assets on grounds that (i) he, Mr Robert Saunders is the main breadwinner; this remains the case as whilst Mr Saunders was forced out of his previous job due to ill health caused by extreme stress for a brief period of time, he is now working full-time again; (ii) secondly, your own input into the joint account is both erratic and therefore unreliable. We concur with Mr Saunders that your inability to run the home or look after your offspring in a correct and orderly manner (we understand it is not unusual for you to take the children, and your pets, with you to your place of work), adds additional strength to his case.

We are to advise you therefore that Mr Saunders is claiming full custody of the children due to your diminished responsibility. When this is granted by the courts, we shall endeavour to arrange access to your children for you, albeit on a limited basis.

We conclude therefore by stating that it is obviously in the best interests of all parties concerned, in particular your two children, that this matter is dealt with and concluded as swiftly and as amicably as possible, with which we feel sure you will concur bearing in mind the tender age of your two offspring.

We would point out that this naturally and inevitably involves your arranging immediately for the joint home which you now occupy to be marketed for sale, and that you also arrange the immediate sale of all joint family goods and chattels.

We would like to helpfully propose that as Christmas is fast approaching, the two children complete the term at their current school before relocating immediately to London and into the care of Mr Saunders. We feel you may be comforted by the fact that an excellent school has been located for the children close to Mr Saunders' residence. We feel you may also like to know that Mr Saunders' sister will be on hand at all times to collect the children from school and care for them until their father returns from work.

We should be grateful, therefore, if you would sign and return the enclosed acknowledging receipt of this letter so that we may dispatch the matter immediately and finalise both the divorce and custody as soon as possible thereby allowing the two children to be reunited with their father in the comfort and security of his London home.

We have the honour to be, etc.
Yours, etc.

In her great agitation, Becky had paced from the kitchen through the sitting room and into the hall, staring only once at the letterbox before turning back. She now sat by the sitting room fireplace slumped onto the cold floor, sobbing, softly and sadly. The sobs grew louder and louder until a piercing scream emitted from Becky's throat, the tears flooded down her cheeks and onto her neck, soaking whatever clothing that happened to be in the path of the salty stream.

Maurice shot upstairs like the proverbial scalded cat, whilst Flake and Cadbury howled outside the conservatory door to be let in to see what was the matter with their mistress, and then the telephone began to ring stridently.

"Shit!" screamed Becky.

"Hello," she sniffed a few seconds later.

"Just ringing to check you got the mail, bitch. Sounds like it. Oh, and by the way, don't touch a thing until I say…I'll be down…make sure you're not around." And with that, the line went completely dead.

"Oh, my God," whispered Becky, sinking once again to the floor, her knees making contact with the hard flagstones with a teeth-jarring crack.

A few moments later, she raised her head and narrowed her brown eyes, her normally smiling lips pursed harshly; Becky was suddenly filled with such anger and loathing for her sadistic, creepy husband, that her mind miraculously cleared and she was at once filled with a fierce determination to fight this battle with all the tools available to her.

"My God," she exclaimed breathlessly as the penny dropped, "he still thinks I'm submissive, dithery Becky. Well!" she shouted, "Little does he know!"

And with that, she jumped to her feet muttering fiercely "Right!" before marching purposefully into the kitchen where she grabbed the cooking brandy from under the sink and took a large slug.

Becky then strode across to the conservatory to let in the now soaking wet and very muddy dogs.

"Baskets," she ordered briskly, not caring about the mess.

Maurice was nowhere to be seen.

* * *

Half an hour later, having stood at the kitchen window collecting her thoughts together, Becky marched purposefully upstairs and into the large bedroom she and Rob had once shared.

Throwing open the double doors of the large wardrobe on the far right hand side of the room, she impatiently shoved aside suits, trousers, shirts and jackets hanging there.

"Not taken much, has he?" she muttered.

"Just as I thought," she exclaimed loudly, "they've all gone, he's taken them to London!"

Becky was in fact referring to the now empty space at the back of the wardrobe behind the hanging clothes where once had hung her husband's alternative wardrobe; expensive silk dressing gowns and pyjamas, and gaudy silk scarves, never worn to her knowledge; they were from Rob's past and she never asked about them and had never once seen him wearing any of them.

She sat heavily on the bed for a moment pondering her next move whilst casting her mind back.

"Mm," she hummed questioningly, knitting her eyebrows together and locking her eyes onto a large dangling spider's web suspended above the bathroom door.

Now that's a bit odd...why would he tell Mum he'd taken the photographs...why would he take them anyway, he was never interested, it was me who took all the photos and stuck them in the albums...but I'm sure there's a huge pile of photos in the attic, in boxes I think...maybe he took those...but why? ... maybe just to spite me ...

Deep in thought, Becky rose slowly from the bed and made her way towards the attic door half way along the landing. Cautiously, she made her way up the short staircase to the huge open space above.

"Thank goodness there's lighting up here, at least I can see my way around," she said encouragingly to herself.

The attic was in three sections—the two sections to the left of the staircase were mainly filled with children's toys— a big old dolls' house and a winding car track were amongst the dusty items as well as boxes of dressing up clothes. The children rarely came up here, it was too far away from everything and they found it a bit scary, at least that was what Polly had once told Becky.

However, to the right, partly curtained off, was an area full of boxes, and odd bits of furniture; and at the far end under a small north-facing window, was a wooden bench that Rob used from time to time for carpentry, or so he said because Becky had never seen any evidence, and there was no sawdust anywhere to be seen.

"That's funny," she said to herself, "I don't remember those metal things, they look like stirrups!"

Something crawled into her brain and settled there, an icy thought that wouldn't melt.

She moved gingerly towards the bench as if afraid it would bite. On the left-hand side of the bench was a high wooden stool of sorts with straps attached to it.

"I don't ever remember seeing that piece of furniture either," thought Becky cautiously.

She was just about to turn around and head back to the staircase, when something caught her eye on the floor near the edge of an old dark red curtain draped over what looked like another table. Gingerly, Becky bent down to have a closer look at what appeared to be an old photograph, and as she did she loudly caught her breath and instinctively clutched at her throat and chest as if appealing to the invisible gods of her amulet for help, as there, staring at her out of the photograph was a face she hazily thought she recognised; but she was confused because looking out at her was someone whose face was wreathed in a paroxysm of what could only be excruciating pain, greasy curls stuck to her cheeks.

Fear clutched her racing heart as she slowly lifted the dark red curtain up a little at its edge.

There, behind the curtain, in a dark recess, was a cardboard box. Cautiously, Becky dragged the box out from behind the curtain, sat down on the floor and lifted the flaps. Inside was what appeared to be an ordinary looking photograph album. She exhaled slowly, relieved to find what she thought must be one of the albums Rob must have left behind.

I don't recognise it though, Becky mused as she slowly worked out how to open the mysterious album.

Nevertheless, sitting back on her heels, she gingerly picked the album up and opened it. Instinctively, she dropped the album, a loud gasp emitting from her throat as if stung by a scorpion. What she saw inside made Becky want to pass out.

"Noooooo…" she hissed, throwing the book away from her with force and standing up so quickly that she hit her head on a low roof beam, almost passing out.

"Oh…my…God!" was all she managed to whisper.

The album had fallen haphazardly exposing a double page spread of obscene and sadistic images that danced on the floor in front of her bloodshot eyes. Bending down, she quickly flicked to another page trying to escape the nightmare, but the images merely served to heighten her fear as the terrifying figure in all the photographs slowly nudged her brain into recognition of familiarity. She knew this person whose head was adorned in a variety of crude wigs, the clothes lewd and garish; stockings and suspenders featured in each photograph prominently, ridiculously high heel shoes planted into overlarge feet; and always the hideous background of masochistic instruments—whips, canes, metal chains—some even with barbs.

She looked again feeling desperately and urgently sick as a kind of fever overwhelmed her as her eyes flew from one shocking image to another.

"… *How*?…*When*?…Why*? Why?*… And…Here of all places…How could he?" She hissed.

A tripod stood like a sentinel behind the album in answer to her query, as sliding to the dusty floor in a crumpled heap, the truth hit home at last. There was no one else involved, this was entirely a make-believe world, a ghastly escape. There wasn't another woman, for this was Rob.

Head hanging loosely, flopping about like a sodden mop, Becky heard the telephone ringing as if from a great distance.

Dragging herself to her feet, Becky stood ashen-faced, sad, damp eyes fixed on a deep purple and threatening rain cloud in the sky outside the attic window. In this empty void, she accepted all she had seen, and recognised the truth at last; the penny had finally dropped and come home to roost; all the pieces of the jagged jigsaw puzzle fell neatly into place. She knew now, beyond a shadow of a doubt, what had really been happening in those dark days after Rob lost his job and retreated into dark, lingering depression. He had escaped, up here to the attic, to live another existence in a fantasy world beyond Becky's wildest imaginings.

A clear mental picture flashed into view of her flying visit to the attic in the summer, lumping up the stairs the heavy album of family photos that had been lying in the downstairs hall; she remembered how just before her parents arrival in the summer before they left for France, she had spun about the house like a whirling dervish, dusting, tidying, cleaning—so fast did she spin that she was completely blinkered to the array of macabre items lying around like hideous marionettes waiting for the master of ceremonies to bring them to life.

Becky now saw how it must have been that on his brief visit to the house in the summer, in such great haste was he to remove all photographic evidence of his secret life, that Rob had snatched up the wrong album.

He can't have looked at the album, thought Becky suddenly, *or else he would have been down here again like a ton of bricks ... or he must have hidden it well out of the way ... until he's sorted living arrangements with Chloe maybe ... mmm...* and at that her thought processes exhausted themselves as an image of a large glass of brandy appeared.

I need to think about this all very carefully and very clearly, she said to herself before she gingerly made her way back towards the attic stairs.

Halfway across the attic space, Becky suddenly stopped, her right hand clutching her throat tightly as it dawned on her like a bolt of lightning, that actually Rob had looked at the album he'd taken to London and that he was coming back to collect his secrets.

* * *

Becky fought to gain composure as she stood stiffly by the sitting room fireplace, clutching a large glass of brandy in one hand whilst the other gripped the mantelpiece for support. Her knuckles gleamed a ghostly white.

"Why did I never suspect anything was going on up there?" she whispered harshly.

Why should you have suspected anything? An indignant inner voice replied. *You were frantically trying to keep things on an even keel for the children's sake, for the sake of the whole family.*

*Yes, but I did sort of know that Rob was a bit different...I just hoped 'it' would go away...maybe that's how he came to hate me...*she thought weakly.

Yes, well, you did fall into that one didn't you? Never marry on the rebound, isn't that what everyone says, isn't that what your mother said...?

Yes I suppose so...but how was I to know? I'd no idea that this was what he was really like. It just never occurred to me...he always did have a filthy temper though...but I always thought it was something I'd done when he shouted, that it was my fault, whatever it was, and I always got confused by that ...

Well, now you know differently, don't you? You have to face up to reality. If you start to weaken now, just remember the one and only time he came home for the weekend after running off to London, all he wanted to do was to boast to you about the caning he'd got from a prostitute—he was proud of that and even told you how much it cost which, if you remember, was five times your weekly food bill!

"Yes," whispered Becky to herself, remembering how shocked and shaken she'd been at the time. "I think I just shovelled that one away, too much to contemplate with everything else that was going on."

Half an hour later, Becky set down the now empty glass on the soot-speckled grate, and sighed deeply. She had been thinking long and hard.

"List!" she said loudly, with a firmness she did not feel at all, at the same time frowning blankly in the direction of

Flake, Cadbury and Maurice who by now had crept to the doorway between the kitchen and the sitting room and lay prostrate staring at her with unreadable expressions, front paws neatly in front of them.

Taking a very deep breath, she said firmly, "Number One—ask Leo for the name of a really good solicitor!"

I won't ask Daddy she thought quietly. In fact, I won't tell them anything, yet…although I'll have to mention the divorce of course…

"Over and above all else," Becky announced loudly, "is the happiness and security of the children, and you three of course," she said looking down kindly at the animals. "And that means securing this house for us, in spite of what may happen between Pierre and myself. This is our home after all is said and done, and I intend for it to remain that way!"

* * *

"Hi, Leo, it's Becky. Yes, I know it's my day off. No, I'm not asking for a pay rise. Leo, please listen, no, don't interrupt. I urgently need a solicitor, the very best in fact. Yes, I did say solicitor, and I need one who deals in family matters…and divorce. And, yes, I did say divorce, Leo. Things have burst like a huge boil. I'm not being disgusting, Leo, you've no idea what's been happening and I really need your help. What? Right now? Of course, if you're sure you can …" Becky was going to say "… spare the time," but realised her last words had been spoken to a void because Leo had slammed down the receiver and was already on his way.

I can't believe this is really happening, gasped Becky.

The front door bell rang long and loud announcing the arrival of Leo.

"That didn't take you long!" gawped Becky as Leo swept in like a hurricane.

"Well, no time like the present! Time and tide wait for no man!" he huffed throwing thick coat, hat, gloves and scarf at Becky who immediately dropped them in surprise.

"Lousy reactions, woman. You'll need to sharpen them up, you're going into battle, remember?"

"Er, yes, Leo, thanks so much for…"

"No time for drivel, let's get on with the task in hand. Found a…"

"Hang on a moment, Leo," interrupted Becky, taking charge. "We can't do this standing in the cold hall, come on in to the kitchen, at least it's warm in there," she finished, as she lead the way through the sitting room into the kitchen and towards the chair by the aga.

"Black coffee, please, if you're making it," ordered Leo briskly, sitting in the chair with a thud.

Kettle in hand, Becky turned open-mouthed towards Leo.

"Don't say a word, just get on with it, for Chrissake," muttered Leo moodily and quite rudely.

Becky had reason to be open-mouthed for she had never heard Leo say the word 'please' before, ever!

It was strange to observe her boss away from the familiar surroundings of the office, and although Leo was gruff as ever, his presence was somehow comforting and reassuring; a bit like a faithful dog, utterly dependable and trustworthy, Becky mused, pouring boiling water onto the dark brown, almost black grains of coffee.

"Bloody hell," growled Leo as he finished reading the letter from Rob's solicitors that Becky had given to him to read. "Your slate had better be pristine, my girl, these buggers are notorious for winning tough cases for their clients."

"How'd you know that, Leo?" Becky dared to ask.

"What? How? How d'you think?"

"I've no idea," she replied candidly, a look of total innocence on her face.

"Hands free!" said Leo abruptly. "How else?"

"Oh yes, of course, I see…"

Which she didn't, at all.

"Enough rabbiting around, Becky, let's get down to business. Notepad? Pen? Good, now, here's what we do …"

* * *

"Pierre!" shouted Becky loudly into the mouthpiece, "How wonderful to hear your voice! Is everything OK?"

It was unusual for Pierre to ring mid-week and Becky had a momentary flash of panic that something must be wrong.

"*Non, non, tout va bien,* Becky, except *ma femme*, my wife, she is being, how you say, *tres difficile*, about our arrangements for *Noel*…she is not 'appy at all…but that is 'er problem, *n'est pas*! *Mais* she wants to come and see *les enfants* on the Christmas Eve which as you know is our day for Christmas *en France*. I told 'er that you would be 'ere and your children also. She is not 'appy but still she come. It could be *un peu difficile* for you Becky, *n'est pas?"*

Becky sighed deeply before replying soberly,

"Er, well, no, not at all actually, Pierre, not difficult for me at all, you see I have big problems over here and so we would not have been able to come over to you for Christmas anyway."

"Mais non!" said Pierre emphatically.

"Mais oui!" responded Becky glumly. "I was hoping to have a chat with you about it at the weekend actually. So, there we are, I'm so very sorry, Pierre. I have no choice at the moment, I'm sure you understand but the *merd* has hit the fan, everything's in turmoil…yes, I have a legal battle on my hands for custody of my children, so I'm in a bit of a state of shock I'm afraid; as I said, I was going to ring you at the weekend, but you got to me first; it seems that we both have problems, you and I. The children? Yes, of course, they'll be desperately disappointed not be spending Christmas with you all, I've not told them yet. But I'm sure that as soon as the dust settles, as soon as things sort themselves out, we'll be on the first ferry over! Maybe in the summer …" she added as brightly as she could, fighting back the tears whilst feeling a great sadness and a heaviness in her heart.

"Eh bien, Becky, there is nothing we can do *uh,"* Pierre replied unemotionally, stating the stark truth. "No problem, as you say *non? Peut-etre* it is the best way, *Noel, c'est difficile non* for the travelling? I will speak to Patrick-Antoine *et* Francelle *immediatement,* they will be, how shall I say? *tres, tres desole,* me too, *moi aussi*, Becky. But the children will be 'appy to see their *maman*! And we shall make the plans for another visit of you and your *enfants* very soon!"

"Yes, OK, fine, thanks Pierre, for being so understanding, and I'll fill you in another time… sit's been such a terrible day."

"*Ah, ma pauvre, Becky,*" replied Pierre kindly. "*Je comprehends,* give me a telephone when you 'ave a moment. *A bientot!*"

"Oh, yes, goodbye, Pierre, we'll talk soon…"

Postman hauling a sack of post up a hill, in a snowstorm.

December

1 December, Friday

"Oh do hurry up, woman, stop messing about, we're late already!" gruffed Leo, striding down Sherton High Street with fierce speed and determination.

Becky said nothing as she struggled to keep up with him, awkwardly and painfully stumbling over the cobbled pavements in her shiny black high heels. She was breathlessly trying to maintain the air of calm and composure that had taken her hours, in fact days to cultivate in preparation for the momentous meeting that lay ahead.

"Right, stop! Here we are!" shouted Leo abruptly as if addressing a platoon of unruly subalterns.

Becky, concentrating on the cobblestones at ground level, failed to stop in time and rammed her head hard into Leo's back, knocking the breath out of him.

Gritting his teeth until his jaw cracked loudly, Leo turned around and grabbing Becky's right arm, yanked her into an upright stance, whilst fixing her with a withering glare.

"Oh for heavens' sake, Leo," said Becky calmly, tossing her dark glossy locks and holding her head up high; briskly she brushed her fingers down both her arms, before gracefully ascending the three enormous stone steps that led up to the large and imposing carved oak front door.

A highly polished brass plate gleamed in the sunlight announcing to the world that this was the entrance to the mysterious world of Messrs. Fortesque, Bland, Cartwright and Smithers, Solicitors. Below the shiny plaque protruded a round and equally polished brass bell-pull.

"Well?" sniffed a slightly chastened Leo. "Aren't you going to pull it then?"

Becky turned her head slightly to one side, disdainfully glancing down briefly at Leo on the step behind.

"Why, I rather believe that is for you to do, Leo," she replied, before turning her fully composed face back to study the front door, waiting for Leo to do her bidding and for the door to be opened for her.

"Hussy!" hissed Leo, stretching up and yanking hard on the brass doorknob.

Almost immediately, the large door swung open to reveal a smartly dressed young man who smiled cordially as he spoke:

"Good morning, Madam, do you have an appointment?"

"Yes, of course we do, Jeremy, name's in the book isn't it?" Leo said, brushing rudely past Becky.

"Oh, it's you, sir, I'm so sorry, I didn't see you there for a moment," the young man spluttered awkwardly, blushing bright scarlet with embarrassment; truth was he had been so totally fixated with Becky that he'd been completely blind to the fact that she was not in fact on her own and that Leo was standing behind and to one side of her.

Jerking his head up briskly in an attempt to regain his composure, the young clerk stood back to allow the odd pair to enter the vast hallway that served as an impressive reception area.

A set smile on his face, Jeremy briskly ushered Becky and Leo into a large, comfortable reception room that was warmed by a welcoming and crackling log fire.

"Please do take a seat; I'll let Mr Fortescue know immediately of your arrival!"

"Thank you, Jeremy," said Leo a trifle haughtily, whilst Becky turned on him with a brilliant smile saying warmly, "Thank you so much."

Jeremy vanished as if by magic, his cheeks burning red, and Leo merely grunted before sitting down heavily in one of the huge armchairs on either side of the fireplace.

Bending forwards in the chair and placing his elbows on his knees, Leo clasped his hands together as if preparing to pray. He took a deep breath and let his eyes focus on the pale blue and yellow Chinese rug at his feet. Slowly, he raised his head and narrowing his eyes regarded Becky for a moment.

"Now, remember what we said Becky," Leo began quietly, firmly and patiently, "that however tempted you may be to butt in, please for the love of God, let me do all the talking, and I mean all," he continued more loudly.

"You'll only confuse things if you do, and the crucial thing is for James Fortescue to have the exact picture, as it stands right now. Remember, you told me everything, and what I am going to do is tell him the *background* story, black and white, without histrionics."

"No, No, No!" Leo said impatiently, his voice getting even louder, and he raised a hand to stop Becky in her tracks, he could see she was about to interrupt.

"Just wait!" he finally barked.

"Remember what I said. We need to draw your husband out, let him have his say and let him think he's winning. I will indicate to James that there are a few additional, probably insignificant, bits and pieces you're trying to resolve. All we want today is to take the first step, set the stage as it were. OK?" Leo finished more quietly, his voice having risen to a crescendo.

Underneath the gruff exterior, Leo was in fact nursing buds of admiration for his erstwhile secretary which, if Becky did but know, was quite an achievement on her part. He was discovering that fighting Becky's cause was actually helping to smooth his own feathers which had become a little ruffled of late and, although he hated to admit it, a bit battered also by Fizz's ongoing obsession with Pierre. Disdain was no longer a shield; Fizz increasingly retreated to her own secret world and it seemed actively sought to avoid Leo wherever and whenever possible. Vitriolic attacks on his apparent snoring had seen him banished to one of the spare bedrooms.

* * *

"Leo, dear man!" came the friendly greeting from the tall, handsome figure of James Fortesque as he rose energetically from his chair behind an enormous desk. The desk was set in front of a large bay window that overlooked an exclusive courtyard garden.

It was a huge room Becky noted, gazing around in open admiration, taking in the elegant and highly polished walnut table on which stood an exquisite floral arrangement, an elegant chaiselongue upholstered in powder blue seductively embellished a beautiful oak-panelled wall, and a huge and striking oriental rug swam upon highly polished floorboards. The whole room looked and smelled of opulence.

This feels right thought Becky. *If anyone can help me, this man can. Good old, Leo!*

James Fortesque strode over to them both, his hand stretched out in greeting.

"Becky!" beamed Leo, "Let me introduce you to James Fortesque, one of my oldest friends and the very best legal brain anywhere!"

"How do you do Becky" James said, smiling warmly down at her and stretching out a well-shaped and manicured hand. "It's a pleasure to meet you!"

"How do you do!" Becky replied, smiling briefly and returning the firmness of the handshake.

"Leo!" said James, turning to greet his friend, and warmly clapping him on the back.

"James, good to see you too, family well I trust?" replied Leo.

"Yes, yes thank you!" James said, eyes twinkling, before nodding politely: "Now do have a seat both of you. Coffee?" he continued, moving swiftly to his place behind the large desk, finger connecting instantly with an intercom buzzer. Turning, he fixed Becky first with a business-like look, now that introductions had been dispensed with.

"Yes please!" replied Becky swiftly, rising to the challenge of the occasion.

"Leo, I don't need to ask!"

Leo smiled benignly.

I've never seen him so, what's the word?... so, cheerful, that's the one! thought Becky, a grin threatening to break out on her carefully composed features. *I'll bear that one in mind!*

Whilst James gave rapid instructions into the intercom, Leo turned very briefly to Becky and gave her that famous 'now leave it to me' look that she had come to know well, but with a shadow of a wink she noticed.

A smartly dressed woman, in her mid-40s, Becky reckoned, swept in almost immediately, bearing a tray of white porcelain cups and saucers, jugs of aromatic coffee and hot frothy milk, also delicious, rounded lumps of sugar the colour of coconut shell and sand.

Mm, exotic tastes too, I'm liking this more and more, mused Becky comfortably.

"Mrs Saunders, would you like milk and sugar in your coffee?"

"Yes please," replied Becky enthusiastically, "one lump of white and one of brown sugar, thank you."

"Of course," replied the efficient lady before turning to Leo.

"And Mr Thorpe-Forbes, I know it's black and no sugar for you!"

"Absolutely!" replied Leo, looking very pleased. Becky would see how well known he was here. *This should all put her at ease, make her feel a bit happier and a bit more confident,* he thought... *although she's a bit of a minx, plenty of guts up her sleeve!*

"Thank you Beryll!" said James briskly and cheerfully as she retreated, shutting the door quietly behind her.

"Now, down to business," James continued more seriously, turning to face Becky. He was about to speak again and had already opened his mouth to begin asking Becky some questions, when Leo pounced.

"James!" he said firmly, drawing attention away from Becky. "I should like to say that Becky has taken me fully into her confidence and has asked me to speak on her behalf when and where appropriate and to explain the situation to you as regards the breakdown of the relationship between herself and her husband. I know you, of all people, understand how these situations can be emotionally highly charged."

James looked to Becky who smiled and said, "It's fine with me, I'm only too grateful to Leo for all his support."

"Right, Leo," nodded James brusquely, "let's have it."

* * *

2nd December, Saturday

Rob stretched luxuriously, raising both arms above his head and clenching both fists before relaxing his elbows and bringing his fingers together in horizontal prayer mode behind his head. His senses dwelt on the delicious aromas of bacon and coffee that wafted up from the large, warm kitchen below. He had had a late one, drinks in the pub after work before a pre-arranged appointment with Louise. Rob lay back on the soft pile of pillows and contemplated with unadulterated pleasure how vicious and cruel she had been; he had added a few rather naughty admissions to his list of confessions and she had been very angry with him, in fact he had actually experienced a moment of sheer terror when he fleetingly wondered, in the midst of the humiliation, whether she'd lost the plot completely and was actually going to kill him, so vicious was the exquisitely painful beating he'd received.

    He reached down and with his left hand gingerly felt the raised welts that striped his buttocks; he gasped out loud, wincing with pain, then inhaled very slowly through his nose as his whole body flooded with deep, throbbing pleasure. After a while, he twisted his head round trying to see the state of his backside. But it was the large mirror on the wall a few feet away from the side of the bed that showed Rob the true picture. He saw dark red, thick stripes across his buttocks. He also saw dark, thick stripes of his dried blood on Chloe's pristine white, exquisitely laundered Egyptian cotton sheet.

"Bugger," he swore softly.

"Have to bin that one," he said more loudly to himself, as an afterthought.

But Rob soon forgot all about the soiled sheet as, stretching again, he swung his legs over the side of the bed and enveloped himself in the caressing luxury of his thick, dark blue Fortnum & Mason towelling bath robe.

Whistling softly under his breath, he sauntered over to the big bay window that looked out onto the garden. As he gazed, thinking of nothing in particular, a few scattered flakes of snow began to fall gently out of the charcoal grey sky.

Perfect day for staying in, he thought to himself.

Those solicitors 've got it all stitched up so I might as well just relax a little...start taking the covers off everything in the basement, ready for the kids, and...why not give myself a treat... And his thoughts wandered to the box of explicit photographs hidden discreetly in the basement. Rob had bought himself a large new bed with a top quality memory foam mattress; the bed had four large under-drawers, and it was at the back of these drawers that Rob planned to keep the photographs, safely stored and hidden neatly behind a panel placed half way back within each drawer. The panel could only be removed by sliding it out of a thin slit half way back on the inside edge of the drawers.

Rob had already made a plan to return the family album he had picked up by mistake when he visited the house in the summer; his plan involved calling at the house when the kids were at school and Becky at work, and swapping the albums; after all, why not, he still had a key. And next Friday would work well, he had the day off.

"Ingenious!" he said out loud to himself, heading off to the shower and a jar of soothing chamomile lotion.

* * *

"Good morning, Chloe!" Rob shouted cheerfully as he entered the large kitchen space, efficiently scooping up the *Daily Mail* from the hall table.

"Oh hi, Rob!" Chloe tentatively replied from the 'business end' of the kitchen as Rob called it.

Chloe never knew these days what sort of mood her brother would be in; he had been particularly difficult lately and quite often unreasonably grumpy. She breathed an inner sigh of relief that for once he appeared to be in a good mood.

"Breakfast's all ready!" she called out.

"Oh great!" replied Rob enthusiastically. "I'm starving, could eat a horse!"

Chloe refrained from making a sarcastic comment that rose unbidden that it was actually pork that they were about to eat.

"Mm," was all she said. "Why don't you sit down, darling, and pour us some coffee?"

"Yip, will do," was the cheerful response. "What are you up … ouch! … to today?"

"Are you alright, Robert, you've gone a little pale?" Chloe asked concerned.

"Fine thanks, just a little sore, must be those piles again …all Mum's fault, it ran in her family, didn't it?…"

"Yes, I know, Rob, but do you mind if we change the subject, we're about to eat you know," she replied briskly, unable to hide the annoyance she felt.

"What? Oh yes, of course, Chlo', sorry," replied Rob penitently, gingerly settling his sore buttocks on the hard wooden chair. "My backside feels like razorblades today."

Trying another tack to alter the course of conversation, Chloe banged a plateful of bacon, eggs, sausages and tomatoes in front of her brother.

"There!" she exclaimed. "Get stuck in!"

Then quickly, before he could say anything more about his discomfort, she smiled brightly down at him and asked, "And what are you up to today? You'll have the house to yourself—I'm out all day with Muriel and Ian. We're off to that new exhibition at the National Gallery, you know the one I mean, the…"

But knife and fork in hand, Rob interrupted briskly, "Oh, great, Chloe! That'll be fun!" He hoped he didn't sound too enthusiastic as he was filled with great excitement of the sudden prospect of having the whole house and the whole day to himself.

"Well, yes," continued Chloe a trifle nervously, "it will be, fun that is, I'm sure it will. You'll be OK then?"

"Me?" Rob replied, his mouth stuffed full of breakfast, "why yes, I'll be absolutely fine. I've got loads to do preparing for the kids, so I'm going to start getting everything ready for when they come up for Christmas!"

"You really think it'll all be settled by then Rob?" Chloe asked anxiously.

"Why yes, of course! Why ever not? That solicitor you recommended is absolutely brilliant Chlo, a real bull dog if ever there was one, and he's pretty certain we're bound to win, no problem!"

"Oh that's wonderful news, darling," replied Chloe enthusiastically, "and it will be so lovely having your adorable two here, and for Christmas! It means so much to me, Robert, after all the terrible traumas this year. I only wish Hugh was here to be able to enjoy it all," she finished wistfully and a little tearfully.

"I know, Chloe," said Rob gently, placing his hand over hers and giving it a quick squeeze. "But things really are working out now as they should after everything that's happened this year, and I can't tell you how eternally grateful I am to you for all your kindness and generosity—I just don't know where I'd be without you," he finished, sniffing back his own salty tears that threatened to flow.

* * *

4 December, Monday

"It's not looking good, girl," said Leo quietly as Becky sat down at her desk.

"What'd you say?" she asked sharply, looking up and fixing Leo with an icy glare.

"I said," hissed Leo sarcastically, "that it's not looking good."

"What's not, Leo? The figures you mean? But I went over them with a toothcombe again yesterday..." retorted Becky, busily scrabbling around in her desk drawer to find her copy of the figures.

"No, not the figures, woman!" shouted Leo, "Your divorce proceedings I mean!"

"Oh my God, what?" Becky gasped.

"Sit down," he said wearily, "here's how it is..." he sighed, examining the nails of his right hand intently, not wanting to see the expression on Becky's grief-stricken face.

Jerking his head up suddenly, Leo fixed Becky with a grim look.

"Spoke to James at the weekend...and it seems...no, do not interrupt me...and it seems your husband holds all the cards; it seems you do not have a case. Clearly and simply, he comes out of this clean as a whistle; given the circumstances, you've not a leg to stand on. House'll have to go and…" Leo hesitated here, he could barely bring himself to deliver the last piece of ghastly news, "…and your kids will have to go to London…alrightee? Got the gist? Are you listening? Hello! Can you hear me?" He finally shouted by now quite frantic as Becky appeared to have entered a state of catatonic shock, frozen like a lifeless puppet.

Raising his voice to loudspeaker level, Leo continued, "I'm so very sorry, Becky, but it seems there's nothing more we can do. Best get off home now and get ready to tell your kids what's happening. And James said to ring him when you get in and before you pick up the kids. Becky! Did you hear a single word I said?"

"Oh Jesus," groaned Leo, "what the hell are you smiling about? You've gone completely bonkers, haven't you? Not bloody surprised if you had…"

By now, Becky was sitting quite calmly at her desk with a broad smile on her face.

Leo was perplexed in the extreme.

"And now for Phase Two!" she grinned triumphantly, breaking her silence. "Let the battle commence!"

"What?" Leo shouted incredulously. "Have you gone stark staring bonkers, woman? What on earth do you mean? Oh Lord. Becky! Don't you get it? It's over, finished, caput. You lost! Can't you see, Becky?"

"Why, yes, Leo, I do see. I see very clearly!" responded Becky calmly. "From your perspective that is…but haven't you forgotten something? What about my perspective? You're forgetting that you don't know a thing about my side of things. Do you?" She finished loudly and emphatically.

"Your perspective?" Leo roared. "What the hell's that mean?"

"What does it mean, Leo? Well, I'll tell you what it means if you'd only shut up for a moment!" retorted Becky feistily. "What it means is that the game is not over, not by a long way. If you remember…no please do not interrupt me…if you remember, before the first meeting with James Fortesque, I told you there was an unresolved issue,"

"Yes, of course I remember, whatever d'you take me for?…"

"… a very kind, caring person actually," interposed Becky and before Leo could say anything further.

Leo's jaw dropped and he was, temporarily at least, rendered completely silent.

"Now, I'll continue," she stated emphatically. "You hear this, Leo, I have facts not yet disclosed that will turn this case over. No, no, don't speak, just stay quiet and let me finish what I have to say, please! You've clearly forgotten about the 'unresolved issue,' that I have something up my sleeve so to speak!

"God, Leo, could you give me a mug of wine or brandy or something, the way you're looking at me just now is freaking me out. I need you to hear what I have to say! OK?"

"What?" Leo replied, shaking his head as if trying to cast off an invisible web. "Brandy, whisky, gin, wine," he muttered, "you name it."

"Oh, in that case," replied Becky feistily, "I'll have a glass of dry white wine with a shot, large one please, of cognac in with it! OK! And why don't you get one for yourself too, you look as if you need it!" she added cheekily.

A clearly shaken Leo rose abruptly from his chair, sending it flying backwards into the wooden office entrance door. Taking no notice of the four spinning wheels of the chair's feet, he grabbed two large crystal tumblers from the office drinks cupboard, and proceeded to carry out Becky's orders to the letter; this included the same for himself although the brandy and wine were in equal measure!

"Right!" said Becky firmly, raising her glass as if toasting success, "Here it is…"

And she proceeded to give, in graphic detail the complete picture to Leo. After the first ten minutes, Leo shot up to refill his glass, skilfully replenishing it without for a moment taking his eyes off Becky.

When Becky at last finished her tale, Leo remained completely speechless for at least two long minutes.

Becoming concerned, Becky asked, "Are you alright, Leo?"

"What? … yes … thanks … fine … just a little shocked and shaken, I've never heard of anything like this before in my whole life. Why the hell did you put up with him for so long?"

"Good question, Leo," replied Becky thoughtfully, searching the depths of her drink for a suitable answer to give. But answer came there none.

"I think everything that's happened this year has kind of unravelled the whole sorry tale…make a good book though don't you think?" She added enthusiastically.

"You're barking mad woman, you know that? A book? How d'you think your kids'd feel having a mother who wrote sado stories?"

"Oh, only a joke, Leo," groaned Becky. "Give a dog a bone."

"Hmm," was the reply.

"Right then," said Leo airily, coming out of his reverie, "we need to arrange another meeting with James, as soon as possible—Christmas isn't far off, we don't have much time!"

"No, we don't, you're quite right, Leo," replied Becky. "But, well, actually, I have already made that arrangement, I rang him first thing this morning before I left for work, and if it's alright with you I'd like to leave at 11.15, I've a meeting with him at 12!"

"Aay?" Leo squawked loudly, "A what? a meeting? What d'you mean?"

"I mean, Leo, that whilst I am incredibly and eternally grateful to you for all your help and support, this is a meeting I need to do by myself. I'm sure you understand," she finished kindly and firmly.

Silence reigned from Leo's end of the office for a further two, long minutes, before, raising up both hands as if in surrender, he said quietly, looking Becky squarely in the eye,
"Yes, of course I understand, Becky. Of course, you must go on your own. I'm sorry I've just got caught up in it all, just felt so sorry for you and the kids, and so damned angry at that useless husband of yours."

"Oh, thank you, Leo!" replied Becky warmly, genuinely pleased and also a little relieved. "I can't tell you what it has meant to me, all your help and support. I could never, ever have got this far without you," she finished lamely, suddenly aware that emotions were running high.

"So, would it be OK if I went in half an hour?" She asked.

"What? Yes, of course, Becky. Why don't you just trundle off now, give yourself some space before your meeting? The bottles and I will do fine without you for a few hours!"

"Oh, thanks, Leo, so very much!" replied Becky, a big smile on her face. "I just knew you'd understand! Where would I be without you?"

"Under a bloody bus most likely," muttered Leo who had gone a bright shade of pink.

Grabbing her bag, Becky jumped up and sped out of the office, but not before catching Leo unawares and giving him a big hug from behind!

"That's enough!" shouted Leo, but Becky's heels were already clip-clopping down the stairs.

* * *

8 December, Friday

"Mummy! Mummy!" shouted Polly at the top of her voice, tearing across the playground towards Becky, satchel crazily bouncing up and down.

Becky spotted William, miles behind Polly, head bent down, walking slowly towards her, and trailing his satchel on the ground behind him; 'like a little old man' Becky thought momentarily.

"Polly!" exclaimed Becky, happy to see her daughter's beaming face. She held out her arms and Polly threw herself into them, chest heaving as she gulped air in hungrily. Becky could see that her daughter was simply bursting to tell her something extremely exciting and of gigantic proportions.

Becky cast a swift glance in William's direction, a stab of fear causing her heart to miss a beat. *I wonder what's wrong...*, she thought anxiously, before turning her full attention back to Polly who was now jumping up and down.

Becky smiled at Polly and said "Now young lady, just calm down a minute, what's been going on today? Let me guess…you came top in English?…"

"No, no!" shrieked Polly.

"Er…oh I know!" guessed Becky, "You had chocolate sponge pudding and chocolate sauce for lunch!…or…"

"No, no, no!" interrupted Polly excitedly. "Daddy was here, he came to see me and William! And we're going to London for Christmas, and we're going to see Father Christmas and the reindeers!…"

A sharp intake of breath involuntarily escaped Becky's throat before she could stop it.

"Whatth the matter, Mummy? You gone all pink…and Mummy, you look very cross…"

Becky said nothing, she was stunned by Polly's news, completely zapped into silent and instant fury.

How dare he? She very nearly hissed out loud, stopping just in time as William at last sloped up to join them.

"Wills darling," Becky said kindly, though through gritted teeth, "there you are!" She bent down to give him a hug, but he just stood there still glumly looking down.

"Wills, what's the matter? Don't you feel well?" Becky continued gently.

"He snot…" Polly was about to intervene loudly, but she was stopped short by Becky who thrust her hand up sharply, eyes still fixed on William.

"Wills? What's up?" Becky continued, reaching out to take Polly's hand, giving it a gentle squeeze.

After still no response from William, Becky straightened up slowly, and taking a small hand in each of her own, walked slowly but resolutely back towards the school house, against the outgoing tide of children heading for the school gates.

"Where we going, Mummy?" Polly asked a little nervously, looking up at her mother's stern face.

"To see the headmaster!" Becky unintentionally snapped.

Polly began to sniff and then hiccough as she ran to keep up with her mother's strident steps.

There was still no sound whatsoever from William.

"Right! Here we are," puffed Becky breathlessly, as they came to a grinding halt outside the headmaster's room.

"Now, you two stay put, sit down here and wait for me, I won't be long…"

And with that, she threw open the door and stormed into Mr Faulkner's office like a whirlwind, not bothering to knock.

"Exshcushe me!" squawked a thoroughly ruffled headmaster, spraying froth all over the papers in front of him on the desk.

"Wash do you shink you are doing Mishes…whatsh your name, who are you?" He carried on indignantly, standing up quickly, and wiping his frothy mouth with the back of his hand.

A thought flashed through Becky's mind that this was an extremely undignified, unheadmasterly gesture. But she let the moment pass, storing it in her memory bank.

"I am Rebecca Saunders, mother of Polly and William!" Becky replied haughtily.

"Well, whash d'you want? You should make an appointment to she me!" Mr Faulkner spluttered rudely.

"Not on this occasion I don't, Mr Faulkner. You see you've breached school rules…"

"Whash!" exclaimed the indignant headmaster, eyes beginning their rapid and opposite elliptical swivelling; Becky experienced instant recall as she now completely understood William's utter fascination with the headmaster at their last meeting with this strange, ebullient figure.

Becky cleared her throat loudly, before continuing, after what she felt to be a very rude interruption.

"… you've breached the rules, Mr Faulkner, by allowing my children's father access to them … he was allowed to enter school and meet with them without my permission and when I was not present! No, No, No! let me finish. The facts are, as you well know from the letter my solicitor sent to you… Mm? … not received it yet you say?…" At least this is what Becky thought she had heard him mutter. And he was looking suspiciously sheepish.

"Not possible, I'm afraid. The letter was sent on Monday, by Special Delivery, so you will have received it on Tuesday … and today is Friday, no?"

Silence fell upon the stuffy, dimly-lit room. Mr Faulkner had been about to say something insulting to Becky to throw her off the scent, like threaten to call the police, but thought better of it. You never knew with these domestic traumas, and it looked as if his suspicions were right, that this woman was clearly unbalanced. And he had quite warmed to the polite gentility exuded by the husband when he turned up unexpectedly at lunchtime, asking to see his children because his wife had been keeping them from him. The headmaster had softened and allowed the meeting to go ahead.

But Becky's assertive manner together with accurate information about that Special Delivery letter from her solicitor, could not be ignored, but it nonetheless made Mr Faulkner cower like a scolded old dog who had been caught raiding the dustbins.

"Hmmm," was all he could manage, and silence reigned for three long minutes, before he began clearing his throat now filling up with froth and threatening to choke him. He was making strange 'Mr Bean' sorts of noises Becky observed cynically.

"Well?" she said sharply. "I can tell from your silence that you have indeed received my solicitor's letter; it's alright Mr Faulkner, I won't put you through the indignity of having to admit that you have lied to me. It'll be our little secret. But if ever anything like this ever happens again, then be assured I shall be down on you like a ton of bricks!"

"Erhemmm…" croaked Mr Faulkner and gingerly cleared his throat as if it was lined with glass.

"No, don't speak!" ordered Becky, still fuelled by her anger and in the knowledge that whatever happened now, all hell was being let loose.

Mr Faulkner merely gawped at her, open-mouthed, white froth gathering at the edges.

"I am going to reiterate what the letter legally requested, which is that under no circumstances are either Polly or William to be allowed access to their father until further notice. Do I make myself clear? I hope that by now you have got that message Mr Faulkner. Mr Faulkner?" Becky finished, by now a bit disconcerted by the pallid expression of what appeared to be shock on his face.

"Why, yesh, of coursh Mishish, er. Shaunders. Quite, quite…" he spluttered at last.

"Good," replied Becky curtly, at last satisfied that she had got the message across and that what had happened today would not happen again. Then turning abruptly, she grabbed the knobbly old black door handle and yanked open the door, saying very loudly, "Good day to you!" without a backward glance.

As she slammed the door behind her, she looked down triumphantly at two upturned little faces, staring at her with identical expressions of surprise. Polly and William had no idea what had been going on in there, all they knew was that Mummy had had a good go at Mr Frog. She was a hero, although they couldn't understand why except that perhaps it had something to do with Daddy turning up out of the blue today. Polly had been so happy to see him, and William had too to begin with but had clammed up when Daddy had said all the stuff about going to live in London. He didn't like that, what would happen to the dogs, and Maurice, and his den, and what about Mummy?

Polly was excited about everything, it seemed he was the only one who just didn't understand what was happening, and this made the guilty feelings he already had even worse. *Daddy had seemed different*, Wills thought, *not quiet any more but talkative and a little stern. And then Mummy was really cross. I must have done some really, really awful things,* thought William, *maybe if I'm just quiet, it'll all go away, and Mummy and Daddy will love me again…*

Once the children were safely in the car, Becky turned around and said, "How about pizza and chips in front of a big cosy fire with your favourite film? Special treat! No, Pols, I know what you're going to say, but it's William's turn to choose, isn't it?" she finished, smiling kindly at Polly, before giving a sideways glance at William who was now staring out of the window with a blank expression on his face.

"Oh, OK!" replied Polly brightly. "Willium, what film shall we watch?"

"Spiderman," he replied dully not moving his head.

Becky stoked up the fire and threw on two more chunky, aromatic pine logs, sending sparks flying up the chimney like rockets on bonfire night. A glowing bottle of smooth red Bordeaux stood open and breathing on the granite grate, a large glass at its side.

Crouching down on her haunches, Becky stared for a while into the fire, eyes locked in sub-conscious space, mesmerised by the flying sparks;

Just like stars in a dark sky, she mused, coming back from wherever she'd been. *There certainly is light in the darkness but you have to fight to keep the flame burning, you just never know when something or someone might try and snuff it out ...*

Rising slowly, Becky bent down and poured half the bottle of the red nectar into the glass. Holding it up in the air, she spoke to the glass of wine softly—"Cheers!"—before taking a protracted sip. Becky placed her glass of wine carefully onto the grate and padded over to the telephone. She picked up the handset and carried it to the sofa in front of the fire; it just about reached. Sofa at her back, Becky sank down onto the rug, and dialled her parents' number. Just as Becky's hand reached her glass of wine, Lisa answered:

"Mum, it's me," said Becky quite softly, taking another large sip of her wine.

"Darling! How lovely to hear from you! How are you all? How exciting to think it's really not long now until...?"

"Mum, please, hang on a moment, I've got something to tell you. No, everything's fine, it's just there's been a change of plan. Look, I know how much you and Dad are looking forward to coming over here for Christmas, but, if you don't mind that is, we'll be here too…there's just so much going on, what with the divorce and everything, that I just need to be on the spot. And of course, there'll still be plenty of room for us all…I know it won't be quite the Christmas you'd planned, you know, peaceful and, well, civilised. But it might be quite fun, don't you think?"

"Becky darling, no of course we don't mind in the least. How wonderful, and what fun it'll be! Is everything alright though? You sound a bit, oh I don't know, a bit subdued?"

"I'm fine thanks Mum. Just got a lot on my plate at the moment. It's quite a relief actually not to have to make that massive journey, and at this time of year when the weather can be appalling…I must've been mad to have ever contemplated it!"

"What about Pierre? You seemed to have become quite fond of each other… and Polly and William are always talking about Patrick-Antoine and, oh what is her name, the little girl, I never can remember it?"

"Francelle, Mum, she's called Francelle. And everything's fine on that front too. I am just being realistic these days … let's say my eyes have been opened to quite a lot of things lately, and by no means all involving Pierre, in fact he's been the least of my worries!"

"Oh that's good, darling, sorry for asking, Daddy and I do worry about you sometimes. But I'm so glad you're sounding so positive, and calm too, more like your old self, before … well, you know what I mean!" Lisa finished a trifle lamely, embarrassed to admit even slightly that she'd always had her misgivings about Rob.

"Oh, I know what you mean alright Mummy! Listen, we'll have all the time in the world to catch up properly very soon, it's only a couple of weeks until Christmas, and I can't wait!" Becky said breezily. "Just longing to see you both. You're all arriving on the 23rd aren't you? What? Oh, yes of course, Gina and Robin arrive on the 24th."

Becky didn't want to talk too long or in too much depth with her mother tonight, she needed to hold on to her hard-won peace and calm, allow it to 'bed in' like a plant in the soil. And she felt an energising sense of certainty and determination that was new. Tonight, she would allow herself time to relax and unwind by the fire. She would phone Pierre tomorrow evening, time to pull that plug too she thought caustically taking a pensive sip of her wine. Narrowing her eyes and holding up her glass to watch the flames enhance the colour of her wine;

"Bastard," she whispered vehemently. "Bloody little, lying shit," she said out loud.

I remember quite clearly, she thought, *wondering what it was about the relationship between Pierre and his so-called 'help' that made me feel ever so slightly uneasy...but then I forgot about it, didn't I and instead allowed myself to become mesmerised by his charm, devastating good looks and seductive ways...poor Fizz, she's been taken in as well, hooked like me by a sexy French libertine...wonder if it's affected business...must try and remember to ask Leo some time...*

...and tomorrow I shall devote all my time to Polly and William—we'll all go for a long muddy walk with the dogs—and we'll walk and talk, and be happy...I shall keep an especially close eye on them both from now on...

Finally, all troubling thoughts put to bed, Becky breathed in deeply, inhaling the aromas of the warm red wine and the crackling pinewood. She felt a huge sense of peace enfold her like a cloak of knowledge and protection. She knew there were still huge hurdles to overcome, but she knew in her heart that she was on the winning side now that the balls were beginning to fall into her court. She instinctively knew that all would be well, now that she had found herself again, retrieved her natural courage.

9 December, Saturday

Dappled sunshine gently rippled over Becky's face, waking her from a long and peaceful sleep. The house was silent as if also resting. She stretched luxuriously, wallowing in the recognition of Saturday morning, no need to rush, no work, no school, just a glorious day ahead that she hoped would be filled with the 'shape of things to come.'

The children must be exhausted, she thought. *What a horrendously difficult time this is for them. I'm just so relieved that my strength and resolve have returned…*

"Mummy!" whispered a little voice, "Are you 'wake?"

"Yes darling, I am, come on in and cosy up Pols," replied Becky softly and sleepily, holding her arms out to Polly who stood in the bedroom doorway, thumb in mouth and teddy bear trailing the ground behind her.

"Why's Will still asthleep Mummy?" Polly whispered.

"I expect he's tired, darling, don't you?" Becky yawned.

"Yeth, I think he is," replied Polly pensively as she shuffled over to the big bed.

Cuddling up to her daughter, Becky was reminded how long it had been since they had done this. A flash of concern about William flipped her heartbeat for a moment.

He'll be fine, she assured herself, *I'll make sure of it. We'll have a lovely day altogether and I'll explain what's going on…I hope they're not too disappointed we're not going to France for Christmas…*

Becky and Polly lay for a while together, Becky gently stroking Polly's forehead as if trying to wipe away all worry that must be going on in her little mind.

"Shall we go and wake Wills, then have breakfast in our pyjamas?"

"Oo, yeth, let's!" squeaked Polly, eyes opening wide.

They padded out of the bedroom and headed towards William's bedroom just a little way along the landing.

Gently knocking first, Becky and Polly opened the door, chiming together loudly, "Surprise! It's Saturday!"

A muffled sound came from underneath the Spiderman duvet.

"Wills! Wills!" shrieked Polly loudly, "Wake Up!"

"I'm going downstairs to make bacon and eggs for breakfast!" announced Becky brightly, leaving the children to themselves.

Half an hour later, lured by the delicious smells wafting upstairs of bacon frying in the pan, William and Polly zoomed breathlessly into the kitchen.

"Weeeeee!" shrieked Polly very loudly, sending Maurice flying out of the kitchen like the proverbial scalded cat, and jolting Flake and Cadbury abruptly out of dog-dreamtime—they immediately began thudding their tails energetically like drums on the edge of their basket and barked in unison!

Becky was suddenly overwhelmed with feelings of great joy at the lifting of the dark cloud that had been keeping their lives in a constant state of 'greyness' for so long; but these happy feelings were also tinged with great sadness that Rob was no longer here to enjoy this, to be with them all, but he had made his choice and they now had no choice but to accept this; sadly this is a shadow the children will carry for the rest of their lives…

"Boots!" shouted Becky loudly from the conservatory where she now stood waiting for Polly and William, the dogs excitedly milling around, wagging their tails and panting in anticipation of an adventurous walk.

"Here we yar Mummy!" squealed Polly, jumping up and down.

It had begun to snow, a few white flakes falling softly from the blue-grey sky.

"Wills!" called out Becky and Polly in unison.

A loud sniff announced his bedraggled arrival as he shuffled through from the kitchen in odd socks, jeans and pyjama top.

"Wills darling," said Becky gently, "don't you want to go for a lovely walk? It's snowing!" she finished brightly.

Another sniff was all the reply she got.

"Oh dear" sighed Becky, taking off her gloves and boots.

"Polls, you wait her a minute with Wills, I'm just nipping upstairs for some warm things. Wills darling, look!" said Becky as she passed William, her hand resting on the top of his head gently, smiling down at him, "It really is snowing! Won't be a mo."

A few minutes later, Becky returned bearing warm hat, gloves and jumpers.

"Now!" she said brightly, kneeling down in front of William, "Let's put these on then off we go!"

Standing up, Becky opened the conservatory door and they all stepped outside into the whitening world; with the dogs bounding ahead, she took a small hand in each of hers and smiled down encouragingly and lovingly at William and at Polly.

"Now! Where shall we go?"

"Old tree, the old tree!" shrieked Polly excitedly, jumping up and down.

"Right!" replied Becky, laughing. It was their favourite place of all, and they set off up through the old orchard and out into the paddock at the top. The 'Old Tree' stood down below the big field beyond the paddock.

Polly let go of Becky's hand and danced ahead, snowflakes swirling around and about her.

"Wills, do you want to run around too?" Becky asked brightly.

Wills looked up at her with such an expression that it jolted Becky's heart for it was a look that would have better suited a little old man, a sad little old man at that.

"Okay" he replied quietly, before slipping her grasp and running on ahead.

That's better, thought Becky, sighing deeply. *Give him time poor little boy…only I just hope what I've got to say to them doesn't drive him further into his shell…*

Twenty minutes later, with the snow now settling properly on the ground, Polly, William and Becky arrived at the old oak tree which despite the weather still had a dry, sheltered area around its base.

"Look! I've brought a rug to sit on, and…"

"Mummy! Mummy!" squealed Polly, "Have you got a nicpic?"

"Yes! well as a matter of fact I have!" laughed Becky and she set down an old tarpaulin onto the ground before covering it with her old school tartan rug. She opened the backpack she had been carrying and laid out the feast in the centre of the rug which, although nothing like as elaborate as the contents of Ratty's hamper in the Wind in the Willows story, it was exciting and exotic to her two hungry children; there were chocolate biscuits, tangerines, marmite sandwiches, some crisps, and mugs of delicious, frothy hot chocolate.

Flake and Cadbury bounded up hoping for treats, but then a pheasant calling stridently from a nearby thicket, set them racing off again in hot pursuit, picnic scents lost and forgotten, for the moment at least!

After filling their mugs again with hot chocolate, Becky sat back against the solid trunk of the gnarled old tree, smiling gently at her two children, mouths now covered in chocolate as they munched happily and contentedly.

Not wanting to spoil the fragile peace, Becky let the silence rest over them. A moment or two later, however, William surprised her by asking very clearly, "Mummy, are we going to France?"

"Why ask Wills?" Polly said indignantly.

Becky seized the moment as, taking a sticky hand in each of hers, she said, more brightly than she felt; "...well, funny you should ask that Wills because it's something I wanted to talk to you both about today anyway...now, I know how much you've been looking forward to Christmas in France, but I'm going to suggest something much more exciting!"

Both children gasped exaggeratedly in anticipation.

"First of all," resumed Becky, "Father Christmas wrote to me the other day to say he's very much looking forward to visiting us again this Christmas and that he hopes that the mince pies will be as delicious as they always are! And that the reindeer are particularly looking forward to their carrot and hay break and a rest-up in our barn!…"

Both children were speechless, looking with awed expressions on their faces over the fact that Father Christmas had written to their Mummy; and then the penny dropped— "But Mummy! We won't be here…" they both wailed in unison.

"Ah, but yes…" replied Becky mysteriously, holding her right forefinger against her right nostril. "Now this is a secret …we shall be here, at home, when Father Christmas comes to call on Christmas Eve with his reindeers, and you will be tucked up in your own little beds with sugar plums dancing around your heads! "

Becky let that sink in a little before pressing on.

"…and the day before Christmas Eve, granny and grandpa are coming to stay and so we can all decorate the biggest Christmas tree we can find together… and then on Christmas Eve, we'll have a big party and you can invite all your friends …"

Both children were now clearly excited, gasping at each new revelation.

Then Polly broke the spell by asking, "Mummy, I thought we was going to France?"

"Well," replied Becky swiftly, "we were, but now we're not, things are different and I have decided that we, the three of us, need to be in our own home for this special Christmas…besides we might get held up by bad weather if we went and that wouldn't be as warm and as cosy as being at home would it? You can speak to Patrick-Antoine and Francelle on the phone if you would like to…"

"Not really," announced William loudly, "I want to be home and hear reindeers on the roof!" he finished with the biggest smile Becky had seen in a very long while.

Her heart lurched as she struggled to hold her composure against a sudden flood of tears that threatened.

"Mummy!" gasped Polly. "Party! Whoopee!" she shrieked, and leaping up she began a crazy dance around the old oak tree. It didn't take long before Becky and finally William joined in, as together they whooped round and round the tree before falling down in a heap on the rug and the picnic!

The snow was now falling more thickly and although she could hear the dogs in the distance, Becky couldn't actually see them. Whistling loudly for Flake and Cadbury, Becky jumped up. "Who's up for building the biggest and best snowman ever? And who's up for bangers and mash for supper?"

Their laughter echoed over the surrounding fields and up amongst the branches of the old oak tree as Flake and Cadbury bounded up covered in snow. Packing up the picnic things, they all made their way happily across the big field towards home.

11 December, Monday

Sunday had been as good as Saturday, Becky mused, staring out of the office window,

"Coffee? Gin? Whisky?" Leo barked, entering the warm little office like a tornado.

"What?" Becky squawked, shaken out of her reverie.

"Oh, good morning Leo, nice to see you're on form as usual," she said, a trifle sarcastically, although a warm smile spread across her face as she met Leo's kind eyes, his right eyebrow sharply raised.

"Hmm," he replied, "wonder what's up your sleeve this bright Monday morning. Amazed you're here given all the snow we had at the weekend."

"The main roads are clear actually," replied Becky brightly. "And the kids literally bounced into school…" she added, though more to herself; Becky felt a warm glow as she remembered the happy weekend.

"Hmm" murmured Leo again. "I hope that's a good sign, bouncing spells trouble in my book, always run for cover if Fizz starts bouncing…"

"Good weekend I hope, Leo?" Becky asked carefully, not wanting to tip the delicate balance and so find out what she warily suspected about the state of Leo and Fizz's marriage.

"Mm? What?" Leo grumpily replied as he plonked himself down in his chair and began thumbing through the latest bunch of wine trade magazines sitting in a pile on his desk.

"Oh nothing, Leo," she sighed, turning back to her own paperwork.

Becky had grown fond of this eccentric couple, but since the autumn had intuitively known something was awry and that all was not well; Becky remembered now the shock and discomfort she experienced when she had come across Fizz in the garden when Fizz had revealed a side of herself that Becky never knew existed. Now, a few months later, Becky knew in her heart that 'things' between Leo and Fizz had clearly not improved.

"Leo?" Becky asked politely. "Would you mind terribly if I headed off now to see James? The meeting's not until 12 but I'd quite like to get there early and go through everything, you know, in my mind; I'd feel more comfortable doing that, if it's alright with you that is."

"O' course, Becky," Leo replied kindly, peering at her over the top of his spectacles. His feet were on the desk now and he was clearly relaxed, in the midst of planning next year's wine list.

Head down and focusing again, as Becky passed by Leo's desk on her way out of the office, he suddenly put out a hand, gently placing it on her arm and said, "Sure you don't want me to come with you?"

"Oh Leo! How kind! Thank you, but no thank you, I must do this by myself!" blushed Becky as she quickly disengaged her arm and opened the office door, exiting at speed.

"Mrs Saunders! Becky! Welcome!" smiled James Fortescue striding across the room, hand outstretched to greet her.

"Hello James!" smiled Becky politely, allowing herself to be guided to her chair.

"Tea? Coffee?" he enquired, settling back down behind his large desk, finger on the intercom buzzer.

"Black coffee please," replied Becky, "that would be perfect, thank you!"

Coffee dispensed, James Fortesque immediately began the meeting by making a statement that Becky would never forget.

"Well Becky, I have to say that it looks like we've won the day for you!"

"What? What d'you mean won?" Becky exclaimed, her eyes wide and round, a stunned expression freezing her face and locking her jaw open.

"Really?" was finally all she could say as she mentally struggled to take on board the enormity of what had just been said to her; Becky had been anticipating a long, drawn-out battle.

"In a nutshell, Becky, your husband's case has completely collapsed. Your home is yours, your children are yours. There will be no separation from them. Your husband has requested access to the children, however, and I suggest we grant this, setting out terms of access on, say, a three-monthly basis for example. We can sort these details later but," continued James rapidly and loudly, hoping to jolt Becky out of her shocked state, "but," he repeated, "I must emphasise and reassure you that these visits will be supervised, and the children's aunt, Mrs Hetherington has agreed to be present during the visits."

"Are you alright?" James asked, his eyebrows knitted in concern, "you look a bit pale."

"Erm…no," replied Becky quietly. "I mean, yes, I'm alright, just a little overwhelmed, a bit shocked really I think," she continued, "and surprised, so surprised…"

"Of course, well, of course you are," was the kind response. "After all, it's been a very traumatic and harrowing time for you, for you all."

"But!" interrupted Becky suddenly, "There is something else I need to tell you, about the children, at school, before the weekend…"

"Go on," encouraged James kindly.

"Well," said Becky, sighing deeply as if the whole of life had suddenly become all a bit too much. "Well, on Friday, last Friday that is, when I went to collect the children from school, he, my husband, Rob, had been there, he'd been to the school and he'd seen the children…he'd wanted to take them with him…to London. Anyhow, thankfully, the children were still at school when I went to collect them in the afternoon, but they were confused poor things. So, I marched into the headmaster's office, like a hurricane actually…" continued Becky, glancing up at the solicitor feeling like a child found guilty of doing something naughty.

"Mm," he murmured, nodding at her to continue.

"Well," said Becky, "I actually found out the headmaster was lying to me, he pretended he hadn't received your letter when, of course and in fact, he had."

"We'll keep that one up our sleeve, shall we?" James Fortescue replied. "Thankfully, all is well and your children are safe."

"I have to tell you though," he continued, "that following our recent meeting when you courageously told me about your marital difficulties, the photograph album etc., I contacted someone I know in the Squad in London and asked him to run a few checks, and he in fact uncovered a series of 'assignments' shall we call them, between your husband and a certain, sorry to be so blunt, a certain prostitute who is known to the force for her particular line of work; I, er, understand, forgive me, that violence and cruelty and the infliction of pain is her speciality. It appears from records held by the Met that a close eye is kept on persons working in the sex business, particularly those at the far end of the spectrum shall we say."

James Fortescue paused a moment for Becky to draw breath before carrying on. Becky merely nodded dumbly wondering where on earth all this was going.

"It appears that he, your husband that is, was growing careless and had bragged to a few people in his office about the cruelty and inherent danger involved, and how he got his 'kicks' out of it. The breakthrough came last week," he continued swiftly, noticing the shock registering on Becky's face, "when officers visited your sister-in-law's address; she herself was in fact out but your husband answered the door. The officers in question explained to him that it was not a criminal matter but that they were contacting clients of a certain prostitute, with whom they understand he had links, and whom they had reason to believe was involved in drug trafficking, and was also linked, I'm afraid to say, to child pornography, also abduction."

There was a sharp intake of breath as Becky's left hand shot up to her mouth; she stood up abruptly, and made as if to flee, before slowly sitting down again in her chair, eyes locked harshly onto those of James Fortescue.

Clearing his throat loudly, he continued, "Please forgive me but I am obliged to tell you all this. Your husband has been told the full known nature of this woman's 'work' and I have to tell you that he is deeply shocked and traumatised by all he has learned from the police. And I understand that on Friday, at the school, he just wanted to see his children and to know that they were safe, although he absolutely should not have said he wanted them to go to London with him."

When Becky remained silent, James Fortescue carried on swiftly, wanting to bring things back to the present and the positive.

"However, back to today, and to how things now stand. You are to have full custody of your children; the house is yours and will now be made over to you, although should you sell the property in the next five years, one-third of the proceeds must be paid to your husband. And, at your discretion, your two children may visit their father in London, however, for the time being these visits are to be supervised, by either your sister-in-law or a social worker, or both. I understand that your husband is to remain living at his sister's home; he will be required to undergo psychotherapy for the foreseeable future, which I have no doubt will be of great benefit to him, he is clearly a disturbed and troubled man."

"At some point in the future yet to be determined," James Fortescue continued, "the case will be reviewed as it is hoped that sooner rather than later your children may have as normal a relationship as possible with their father, to enable them to build positively and beneficially for the future."

"What about poor Chloe? Rob's sister? She's not long lost her husband?" Becky stuttered anxiously.

"Mrs Hetherington has agreed wholeheartedly to support her brother through this time, she is a strong, kind lady whom as you know has been through much herself very recently; and it seems that their own childhood trauma, shipped off to boarding school when barely five years old etc, has at this difficult time thankfully worked in their favour and brought them closer together for mutual support and understanding."

* * *

A shattered yet deeply relieved Becky slowly descended the large stone staircase outside the solicitors' office.

Standing on the cobbled pavement below, she slowly pinched herself hard on the thin skin of her left hand.

"Am I dreaming?" she said to herself, raising her eyes slowly to the cloudless blue sky above, her thoughts drifting and spiralling upwards. They were safe!

But then immediately her mind filled with compassionate concern as sad thoughts of Rob filtered through.

"Poor, poor man," she said out loud.

"You alright, love?"

"What?" Becky said, jolted out of her reverie, looking through distant eyes at an old lady who stood staring at her kindly, a bag of shopping in each hand. "Oh, yes, yes thank you, I'm fine," smiled Becky softly.

"Leo can you hear me? I'm in a phone box. Everything's fine, it's going to be alright. I thought I'd let you know!"

"Yes, yes, I can hear you. That's great news!" he bellowed, "You on your way back now, or shall I relent and give you the rest of the day off?"

"Oh, yes please, Leo, that would be a godsend, thank you!—If you're sure that's OK—I'm a bit shell-shocked actually. I'll be in in the morning then!"

"That's fine Becky, just take your time, and I'll see you then! Bye…"

Becky had been going to say thank you again, but he'd gone, in usual fashion putting down the receiver abruptly and without warning immediately he'd finished what he had to say.

Becky smiled, and then momentarily felt a pang of concern for him, things were definitely not improving between Leo and Fizz.

Arriving at the Old Mill House with two hours to spare before she had to collect the children from school, Becky opened the ancient back door and entered her home. The dogs barked madly, delighted someone had arrived to love and feed them. Letting Flake and Cadbury out into the garden, they raced across the snowy grass and up into the orchard, immediately falling upon all the exciting smells that assaulted their sensitive noses. With a deep sigh, Becky filled the kettle and setting it on to boil retrieved her favourite mug from the pine wood dresser, before sinking into the cosy old chair by the Aga.

However, as she sat waiting for the water to heat up, a tiny worm of caution made its presence felt in the depths of her mind, not allowing her to completely relax her guard just yet. This was new territory for Becky and she heeded its hard-won wisdom.

"I'll wait until after next weekend, until next Monday evening, when I know everything is actually signed and sealed; and then I'll tell everyone, and then I'll relax."

Becky was just about to turn off the lights downstairs and head on up to a hot bath and bed, when the phone rang stridently. Dropping hot-water bottle and book loudly onto the hall floor, she flew to answer it before the shrill tone awoke the children.

"Yes?" she whispered loudly into the mouthpiece.

"Cat got your tongue?" was the loud, rude response.

"Oh Leo, it's only you, what do you want?" Becky hissed, secretly pleased to hear his voice. She was wary now and nervous, with everything that was going on, of another threatening call from Rob; she wouldn't feel safe until all those papers were signed as then she would know for sure that all she had learned from her solicitor was in fact true.

"Keep your nose out of the office will you, til after Christmas," Leo slurred, "Take a break, get sorted and I'll see you here 7 January. OK? Got it?"

"Oh!" was all a surprised Becky could say, before weakly adding into thin air because as usual Leo had slammed down the receiver … "Happy Christmas Leo."

Wearily climbing the stairs to bed, Becky noticed she actually felt disappointed that Leo didn't want her back in the office until January, a bit 'put-out', the office and Leo were always a welcome distraction. Becky also wondered fleetingly if all was well with Leo and Fizz; deep down, she sensed it was not.

13-21 December

The next few days flew by in a whirl, as if keeping pace with the dancing white flurries of snow that periodically tumbled out of a blue sky turned suddenly grey. They were only brief flurries however, and salted roads plus an epidemic of Christmas excitement, kept everyone and everything on the move.

Polly and William were totally preoccupied with end of term festivities and excitements, and seemed to have completely put behind them the difficulties and traumas of the past weeks.

"They're firmly 'in the present'," mused Becky as she tucked up first William and then Polly for the night before the last day of term. She hoped and prayed that the children were preoccupied enough not to notice or sense her own inner tensions as she waited like a coiled spring for the letter from James Fortescue that would allow her to breathe deeply and safely again.

Thankfully, distractions were abundant; Becky had swept and cleaned the house from top to bottom, filled the store-cupboards, fridge and freezer with delicious food that Leo's generous Christmas bonus had enabled.

And the day after the end of term, mid-afternoon in fact, Granny and Grandpa were arriving for Christmas; their friends, Gina and Robin Shaw, were not arriving until Christmas Eve.

In the morning, before her parents arrived, Becky had planned a surprise visit for the children to Christmas Wonderland in Crossford, where they could see and chat to Father Christmas, stroke and pat his gentle reindeer, also choose and then dig up their very own Christmas tree which would later be planted out in the garden at home!

In the end, she was extremely grateful that Leo had banned her from the office as she now wondered how on earth she would have been able to do everything that needed to be done in time for Christmas and go to work as well.

Becky also was very grateful for all these distractions as she felt herself to be in a state of suspended animation, waiting for new life to begin.

23 December, Friday

23 December, Friday, dawned grey, misty and cold, at the sight of which Becky's heart fell, her imagination immediately taking flight. It took a massive effort on her part not to slip a large slug of brandy into her morning coffee to lift her faltering spirits.

But there was much to do before the postman arrived, and at least the roads were still clear, although more snow was forecast before the end of the day.

The postman was always a little late at this time of year, but when 3 o'clock arrived and he still hadn't come, and with the light fading fast, Becky couldn't help but feel worried and panicky. She had set her heart and mind on everything being neat and tidy, sorted and organised by today, however, she now felt her plan was fast receding into failure.

Suddenly, the dogs barked loudly and raced towards the front door; but for once, Becky beat them to it as gasping breathlessly she grabbed the wedge of envelopes that appeared as if by magic from the world outside through the large heavy metal letterbox.

"Thank you!" she yelled through the letterbox to the retreating postman.

Thumbing swiftly through the pile, heart banging in her chest, breath coming in short, sharp little puffs, Becky scanned each envelope expectantly, hope fading slowly and gradually until finally extinguishing as she reached the end of the pile.

Biting her bottom lip fiercely until the pain made her squeak out loud, Becky stared blankly at Flake and Cadbury who sat curiously and expectantly at her feet. She had a fleeting sense that both animals knew exactly what it was that she was so urgently waiting for; there was love and compassion in their liquid dark brown eyes.

Breaking the trance, Becky blew both her cheeks out hard, before turning to shout out loudly that it was time for a gin and tonic if anyone was interested.

Answer came there none—making her way back to the kitchen, Becky peeped around the drawing room door to see what was going on, and there she espied four bottoms in the air, two quite large and two very small, crowding around the 7ft tall, very beautiful Christmas tree. Becky cleared her throat loudly, "Everyone alright?"

Four heads turned half way round before turning back again. Without looking up, Polly whispered loudly, "We're looking for the Christmas tree fairies. Shhhh."

24 December, Saturday

Christmas Eve—well, today's the day, thought Becky as she slipped out of bed and padded across to the bathroom where she turned on the hot tap firmly.

It was just 6 o'clock and no one else would be up and about for at least another two hours.

Soaking in the hot, fragrant bubbles, Becky mentally checked her to-do list; it seemed endless and already she felt exhausted at the thought of what lay ahead…presents to wrap, food to prepare, turkey to stuff, house to hoover, house to decorate…party poppers…*Oh my God! the party! I'd forgotten…*

Sinking back down into the deep bubble bath, virtually submerging herself in a futile attempt to escape the day ahead, Becky inwardly groaned,

I just hope that letter arrives; James said it had been sent by Special Delivery but that was on Thursday, and it's Saturday today…oh help, help, help…if only that letter would arrive then I just know everything will be fine, I'll be able to cope with anything, anything at all…

And so it went on, until finally disgusted with herself, Becky climbed out of the bath and standing in front of the mirror, re-adjusted her features so as to present to the world her very bravest face.

It was well past midday when the front door bell rang loudly and insistently.

"That's for me!" shouted Becky, streaking to the hallway with rubber-gloved hands stretched out in front of her. Again, she beat the dogs to it; today however Flake and Cadbury looked thoroughly peeved.

"Now stand back, girls!" she ordered. "Baskets!"

Tails between their legs, Flake and Cadbury retreated, puzzled by the somewhat confusing turn of events that was taking place in their ordered and perfect world.

"Oh! Phew!" gasped Becky throwing open the door and seizing the 'Sign For' sheet. Swiftly planting her signature on it, she snatched the thick, embossed envelope from the thickly gloved hand.

"You awright, Missus?" The kindly, bearded postman enquired, a look of concern on his face.

"Yes!" breathed Becky, a big smile joining her flushed, red cheeks.

"Yes, thank you, I'm fine now" she gasped.

"Thank you so much, you lovely postman!" she said breathlessly, "Happy Happy Christmas to you and yours!"

And with that, Becky thrust both her arms around the now startled postman's neck, and gave him a huge hug.

"Hang on a minute!" she shouted, making him jump.

The postman turned to go, but was assailed again, this time by a crisp £10 note and a bottle of ruby red wine being thrust into his hands.

"Happy Christmas, lovely postman!" she repeated, smiling happily.

* * *

The party, about 12 adults and the same number of children, was due to start at 4 p.m. It would carry on until about 6.30-7 Becky had planned, so that everyone could relax and enjoy themselves before getting home again, with the rest of the evening ahead for final preparations for the Big Day tomorrow!

All the guests had arrived, the adults chatted and relaxed on the sofas and chairs around the large open fireplace in the drawing room. The Christmas tree lights were lit, their reflection twinkling magically in the large patio windows behind, extending the light and joy of Christmas to the garden and the world outside.

Delicious smells wafted from the kitchen, mingling with the fragrant scent of the well-seasoned pine logs burning brightly in the sitting room fireplace where 3 or 4 mothers lay sprawled out on rugs and cushions by the fire, wine glasses raised in unison as Becky bent to refill them with freshly mulled wine.

Becky had just got into a really interesting conversation with one or two of the mums about Mr Faulkner, when the front door bell rang.

Startled, Becky jumped up to answer it.

"I'll be back in a minute," she called over her shoulder.

But she was puzzled and slightly anxious as she made her way to the front door; everyone had arrived and the party was in full swing.

"Please God, don't let it be Rob," she silently prayed, feeling instantly struck down with guilt that she could have such a thought, never stopping for a moment to consider that she had nothing to feel guilty about. After all, her letter had only arrived today ... *maybe Rob hadn't received his and had come here to ... for what? Why would he come here now? ... he hates me I know he does ... I wish I knew why ... but the children, oh my God, of course, he's come to see the children ...*

And it was with all these thoughts spinning around her head that Becky nervously opened the front door of her home on Christmas Eve.

A huge bunch of white roses was thrust into her face so she couldn't actually see who it was standing on the doorstep.

'... Pierre?' she thought in a panic, '... no, no, it can't be, it wouldn't be ... no ... but ...'

"Going to invite me in then or are you going to stand there all night like that?" came a gruff, all-too-familiar voice.

"Leo!" she shrieked, "What are you doing here? How lovely to see you! Come on in! Oh do come in!"

"Where's Fizz?" Becky asked sharply, turning to Leo midway along the hall and causing him to jump.

"Mm? What'd you say?" Leo challenged, meeting Becky's eyes with equal force.

"I said, Leo" replied Becky blandly, "I said 'Where is Fizz'?"

"Mm...rather not talk about her right now if you don't mind" he muttered, "left to spend Christmas with her lot ...you know, the Gloucestershire pile ..."

"Oh!" was all Becky managed. "Better stay here then, plenty of room, food, company, dogs, children...all quite chaotic, it might send you mad you know ..."

Then taking both Leo's hands in her own, Becky planted a big kiss on each of his reddening cheeks, before adding,

"I'd love you to stay and spend Christmas with us, you are very welcome!"

Leo was uncharacteristically speechless for a full long minute before pulling himself together and saying, quite formally, "Thank you very much, delighted to accept, got an overnight bag in the car actually … was going to check in to that Inn at Stokeminster…" he trailed off.

"I wouldn't hear of it, now come on in and meet everyone, you're staying here for Christmas with us!"

Epilogue

Years later, after her book is published, we find Becky, now a very old woman in her 90's, living a Bohemian lifestyle by the beach and near a little fishing village on the Greek island of Seriphos…

* * *

A shaky, wrinkled and slightly mottled nut-brown hand rose slowly in greeting.

"Polly? William? Is it really you? Or am I daydreaming again? Joanna, Joanna, are you there?"

"Here I am Becky, just cooking some lunch for us … I'm sure there'll be plenty to go round," she said aside to herself. Joanna had received the call from the mainland to say they would be on the next boat out of Piraeus. She had given them instructions on how to reach the little villa, which was set back in the shade of overhanging acacia trees but close enough to the white sand and pale turquoise water of the beach for Becky to hobble down for her daily morning swim.

The little village of Livadi was only 2.5 kilometres away, its tiny harbour supporting a small landing bay for passengers off the twice weekly ferry from Piraeus. In the winter months, it was a different matter with one ferry every two weeks, weather permitting, so the few permanent residents never knew whether or not the boat carrying post and messages, and basic food supplies, would arrive or not. But they always coped by sharing and simply making do when the delays inevitably happened. It was both a precarious and a gentle, natural way of life; Becky relished in the peace, simplicity and beauty of the place, and knew all the wild plants and herbs that could be put to both culinary and medicinal uses. She felt free of the bonds of the so-called civilised society she had so willingly abandoned, with its restraints and restrictions, its rules and regulations about what you could and could not do; the winter flu jab blackmail did not apply here; she had her aches and pains but her salve was the sea and the healing herbs. She had never felt so at peace, except for the deep ache in her heart she felt whenever she thought of her children, so distant, so far away, but ever present.

Joanna however had bouts of what she could only describe as cabin fever when the long winter nights and the cold windy weather descended, shutting them off from the outside world. But she rarely complained; she had enormous respect and compassion for her friend and mostly enjoyed their frequent political debates that always veered towards Becky's passion for all wildlife, her growing alarm at what she called 'the greed and stupidity of men'—global warming and climate change, the pointless and outrageous murder of creatures such as badgers, and the destruction of the rain forests …*Soon, we'll not be able to breathe, there'll just be no air left, and we'll either suffer the worst ice age ever or global warming that simply evaporates all the water, and we'll simply burn to death, or suffocate...the dinosaurs all died, and we never know when the same's going to happen to us ... a huge meteor ...*

Becky knew she used to go on a bit about it all, poor Joanna, she was so patient and she did try hard; pity old Bob, her lovely husband, wasn't still around; life had been, she admitted to herself, better then; Bob was always up for a discussion, a good old debate as he called it, and he was always positive; Joanna had always been quieter than Bob, even more so since his sudden and fatal heart attack three years ago.

Becky had come across Bob and Joanna Stapleton when Leo was still alive. Becky and Leo had been visiting Seriphos early one spring and had met and befriended for the whole trip two likeminded people who were as passionate as they were about the Greek Islands and all the exquisitely fragrant flowers and herbs, about the whole way of life. At home, Bob and Joanna lived a hundred or so miles away in Warwickshire, but after that first meeting, every year in springtime from then on, the four of them would meet on the beautiful island of Seriphos where they would spend two glorious weeks walking, swimming and eating, or just sitting on hillsides, in valleys, on beaches, taking in the views and the intoxicatingly scented air.

Then suddenly, with no warning, the Christmas prior to their sixth springtime visit to Seriphos with Bob and Joanna, on Boxing Day, sitting by the fire on the sofa, one arm around Becky, the other nursing a large glass of some ancient port or other, Leo suddenly turned bright red in the face, as coughing thickly he slumped forwards and promptly died, spraying port all over the thick white carpet mingled with his blood.

Becky had screamed, shot out of her seat and dialled 999 before even three seconds had passed. Twenty long minutes later, the ambulance arrived, but it was too late; Becky sat silently weeping on the floor cradling her dead husband's head. There was a post-mortem of course, that revealed not a lot, merely three, cold, dead words on the form, '*sudden burst aneurism.*' These words, and the accompanying images of Leo's death, would haunt Becky for the rest of her life. Her one comforting thought was that Leo had died a happy man and that his life had been extinguished in the blink of an eye; no lingering death for her man, brisk and to the point, as in life so in death…

There was no trip that year to the beautiful scented and sun-baked isle, or for many years to come,

It was a tough year for Becky following Leo's abrupt departure. Complicated legal battles were fought, and in the end, Becky lost them all. Fizz, who was in her mid-80's and in a residential home for genteel elderly persons, claimed her rightful three-quarters share of the proceeds of the Old Manor where Becky and Leo had lived following their marriage, and which had been put on the market within weeks of Leo's death.

At the time of Leo's death, Becky was 60 years of age, and when finally her share of the money from the house sale came through, it was not enough for Becky to buy a little place of her own. So, on the advice of a 'fly-by-night' friend of a friend, she had invested all her money in stocks and shares with the promise of a 'tidy income'; unfortunately, the investments turned out to be completely useless and her money had rapidly diminished, at the same time as a general worldwide stock market decline. And so ultimately, by the age of 65, Becky's circumstances were completely reduced and she found herself in the tiny, damp little cottage living on state benefits, far from friends and family.

Becky became increasingly isolated and depressed, on top of which both Polly and William and their families were by now living on the other side of the world, Polly in New Zealand and William in Australia.

It was at this low point in her life that Becky suddenly found one single, tiny spark of fight within her as she stared bleakly and hopelessly that one cold winter's day, into the dark and lifeless fireplace when she vowed to write it all down.

* * *

The years following the end of this story about one year in Becky's life passed by in a flash; there were happy times and there were sad and difficult times:

Polly and William, having endured the trauma in their young years of their father's virtual absence from their lives—his emotional distance from family life followed by his physical absence when he left for good—were left with deep scars of this traumatic time, and for William especially the guilt he felt weighed heavily on his young shoulders; then there was Mummy and Leo—they liked Leo a lot, he was very kind and was often funny, but he wasn't Daddy. And so it was that their new life gradually took shape, followed swiftly on the heels of the unforgettable Christmas

Eve when Leo had landed on their doorstep with a huge sack of toys, just like Father Christmas himself.

* * *

Polly was a rebellious often sulky 10-year-old and William an uncontrollably naughty 8-year-old when finally their 'new life' began. First they moved from their home to Leo's big old house; it was nice enough, and the garden was OK, but there were no secret places to hideaway in, no magic old orchards for tree climbing, no chaotic and unruly flowerbeds ablaze with colour; there was order, there were straight lines, no vegetable garden or orchard, and virtually not a tree to be seen. Polly and William immediately decided it was all very boring, and despite the fact that their mother was as she had always been, and that she was happy, they now had to share her with a man who seemed to have stepped into their father's shoes without even asking them. They were confused for they neither liked or even remotely understood what had happened, and when this penny finally dropped, then began the long, slow and often painful process of distance gradually and imperceptibly seeping between them and their mother.

Polly and William remained quite close for the rest of their lives. However, the year William turned 23, he and his long-term doctor girlfriend Jan, announced they were expecting a baby and were emigrating to Melbourne; as it happened, a little boy, Rufus, was born one January in London under cold, grey skies, and three months later they were gone, to work and live and love in the heat of southern Australia.

Polly and her Spanish interior designer partner Fernando, first had a little girl, Rosetta, followed two years later by the birth of a second little girl, Jemima; and by the end of that year, Polly, Fernando, Rosetta and baby Jemima emigrated to the south island of New Zealand.

Lisa and Bill, Becky's beloved parents, had faded away one after the other during Polly and William's chaotic teenage years, first Bill, then Lisa. They had been tired and sad at the end.

* * *

The translucent, pale turquoise sea seemed to ebb and flow in time with her ragged breathing; the blue haze seemed to clear for a moment …

"Mummy!" Becky whispered, "Is that really you …?"

The vision faded, as the sounds of the gentle waves lapping on the shore lulled the old lady into a deeper sleep.

She sniffed gently, traces and fragrances of something delicious cooking … was it squid she wondered … Mmm … those wonderful fragrant herbs and the garlic … and then she could hear a splash and a loud hiss, followed instantly by the enticing aroma of red wine. Her tummy rumbled noisily. "Where on earth am I? Mummy are you still there…?"

"Mum! There you are!" a tinkling voice that she knew so well caused Becky to raise her head a little.

"Where did that come from I wonder? I'm sure I heard Polly's voice … Polly?"

Then a deep, warm man's voice, "Hello, Mum, how're doing?"

The mists rapidly cleared from Becky's brain as she jolted back to the present, and there beside her, kneeling on the sand, arms outstretched, big, loving smiles on their beloved faces, were Polly and William.

Becky was speechless for a moment or two before the three of them fell together in a crumpled, tearful heap, laughing and crying.

Lying in bed that night, looking out at the myriad of stars twinkling in the deep, dark night sky, Becky felt a deep peace and calm fill her whole being; her last thought on drifting into her final sleep was that she had loved in her life and was loved in return…and the two children of her heart had never really left.

THE END

The Characters

One Year in the Life of Rebecca Saunders: the characters:

Becky and Rob Saunders and Polly and William, live at the Old Mill House, Little Millston.

Lisa and Bill Copeland, Becky's parents, live at Holly Tree Cottage, Claymoor St John.

Leo and Fizz Thorpe-Forbes live at the Old Manor, Little Beresford.

Mr Herbert Faulkner is Headmaster of Little Beresford Primary School.

Miss Violet Clasby is William's form teacher.

Mrs Hitchens is Polly's form mistress.

Hugh and Chloe Hetherington, live in a big mansion in Richmond, London SW.

Pierre Cipriani and his children, Patrick-Antoine and Francelle, live in Provence at La Maison des Olivieres, Nyons.

James Fortescue, Solicitor, Fortesque Bland Cartwright & Smithers, Sherton.

Mr Edward Pickles, Dentist, Bedhampton.

Bob and Joanna Stapleton (see Epilogue)